Sofie Waits
A Coffee and Donuts Book

Amanda Hamm

ISBN: 978-1-943598-98-4

Also by Amanda Hamm

_____

Said and Unsaid (Coffee and Donuts #1)

The Christmas Project (Stories From Hartford #4)

Collecting Zebras (Stories From Hartford #3)

Jealousy & Yams (Stories From Hartford #2)

Andrew's Key (Stories From Hartford #1)

The 4th Floor Lounge

Meet Cute: 5 Romantic Short Stories

Weathering Evan

1 PRESENT

S ofie gently nudged her friend's arm and watched her eyes pop open. The guilty expression on Amber's face was not an act. She recovered quickly though and made a show of subtly glancing behind her. "I don't think anyone noticed," she whispered.

Sofie leaned closer. "They'll notice the talking though."

"Shh!" Amber put her finger to her lips and her eyes widened as she tried to hold in the giggle.

To make sure she could maintain her own composure, Sofie turned back to the front of the church. She was twenty-two now – they both were – but sometimes when Amber was around she still felt like the little girl she'd been when they first became friends.

Amber kept her eyes open the rest of the mass, but she displayed an exaggerated yawn during the closing hymn. Then she whispered to Sofie again. "We're going to the parish hall after this."

"You mean coffee and donuts?"

"If you're going to drag me out this early," Amber said, "you're going to sit with me while I drink coffee. I obviously need it."

Sofie nodded her consent and they made their way slowly across the courtyard to the hall where coffee and donuts were served between the Sunday masses. Amber pulled a few dollars from her purse and stuffed them into the donation jar before she got in line for coffee. Sofie wasn't much of a coffee drinker, especially not on a warm summer day, so she filled a cup from the water fountain while she waited for Amber.

Amber held her cup in both hands very close to her face. She inhaled so deeply she might have been trying to use the steam as a straw. Sofie thought her friend's devotion to coffee had gotten a bit out of hand recently and she rolled her eyes. Amber smiled and continued to suck in every droplet of the evaporating liquid.

A very stout woman with a cane emerged through the door facing the church. Sofie nodded in her direction. "Your grandmother is coming," she said. "Should we try to sit with her?"

"Naw." Amber shook her head. "She has her church friends, and I'll see her when she comes for dinner tonight anyway." She motioned Sofie to a pair of empty chairs nearby. Two couples were sitting at the table already but facing away from it, towards a handful of young children who were running around with half-eaten donuts in their hands.

Sofie watched the children for a moment and then sipped her water. When she looked at her best friend, Amber was wearing her serious face. Sofie knew this expression well. It was the expression she always got right when she was about to broach an important topic. Amber wore the serious face when they needed to study for a test and when they were about to negotiate which book they would next read together.

Expecting a subject related to wedding planning, Sofie lifted her eyebrows in expectation.

"So," Amber said, "I think it's time for you to tell me why you're avoiding Austin."

Sofie tried to infuse some innocence in her surprised laugh. "What makes you think I'm avoiding Austin?"

"Graduation was a month ago, right?"

"Right." Sofie voiced her confirmation and used her eyes to ask where Amber was headed with that statement.

"And how many times have I seen you since we moved back here?"

"Lots."

"Yeah. Enough to know that you're different when Austin is around." Amber waved her hand between them as though she was somehow assessing this difference.

"Perhaps you only have a vivid imagination."

She smiled and shook her head. "Do you need me to spell out all the things I have *not* imagined?" Amber didn't wait for a response and used one hand to count on the other. "You follow me. There have definitely been times when you tagged along unnecessarily to avoid being left in the same room as Austin. You talk less. Something about you feels guarded when he's there. And then there's today."

Sofie put down her cup and fiddled with the beads on her bracelet. "What about today?"

"Why did you want to come to early church?"

"I told you. Just for a change."

Amber took a sip of her coffee and closed her eyes at the taste. She opened them and immediately put her serious face back on. "You want to know what I think?"

Sofie squirmed. She always felt guilty keeping this secret from Amber. They told each other everything else and now Amber looked dangerously suspicious. "What do you think?" she asked.

"I think you ran out of excuses for not joining the families for lunch after the later mass, and I don't think it's my parents you're avoiding. I think it's my brother."

Sofie tried to look as though this theory was ridiculous. After all, she wasn't avoiding Austin. Not really. She was terrified of spending much time with him – and certainly any time alone with him – and that meant she wasn't going out of her way to see him. But she wasn't avoiding him. "I am not avoiding him."

"Did something happen at the graduation?"

Sofie shook her head truthfully. The insane butterflies that had invaded her stomach at the sight of Austin did not count as something happening.

"Before that?"

"No." Sofie bit the inside of her lips at the less truthful answer.

Amber took another sip of dark liquid and seemed to gather strength for her argument from the coffee. "Something has been weird with you two for a while. I'm not sure when I first noticed it so I don't know how long it's been going on but…"

She eyed Sofie shrewdly. "Did he like ask you out at some point?"

Sofie shook her head again but she felt a hint of betraying color in her cheeks. She told herself she wasn't lying because that wasn't what was causing her tension. Or at least it wasn't exactly what was causing it, or it wasn't entirely what was causing it. He hadn't meant it anyhow. Or maybe he did. But he didn't mean that he was interested. She could say no to Amber's real question.

"Hmm…" Amber continued to study her friend and a slow smile said that she was on to something. She put the cup to her mouth and let the coffee linger over her lips before she set it down again. "Well," she said, "for now we can pretend you're not avoiding Austin. Let's talk wedding."

"Yes to wedding talk." Sofie perked up at the safer subject.

"I'm coming to the shop tomorrow to put in my official cake order."

"We already know what you want." Sofie's parents owned a bakery, and she and Amber had discussed the perfect wedding cake within a week of her getting engaged.

"I only get to plan one wedding," Amber said. "I'm not skipping any of the steps."

"All right. What time should we expect you?"

"Not until after five. Joe's coming with me."

****

Ennemoser Cakes was in a white building with stately columns on either side. The bakery took up the whole first floor and several offices were on the second, the most prominent of which was a divorce attorney. Whenever anyone commented on the unfortunate nearness, Sofie's parents would simply say, "We were here first."

They opened the bakery soon after moving to Thompsonville. Customers were slow to accept the new venture and once they began to flock in, the Ennemosers feared they might still need to close when Sofie's mom, Angie Ennemoser, got sick. But a new manager took up the slack and quickly became a close family friend because of it. Mr. Turner still worked for them but only part time and was talking about retiring now that Sofie was back from school. She was trying to talk him out of it.

The bakery had been thriving the last few years, but Sofie's parents wanted her to have a degree to fall back on just in case. Sofie was optimistic about the shop's future. She went to college anyway because she wanted to feel qualified to help run it and because Amber went to college.

Sofie spent some time on Monday checking inventory before she successfully piped a pink frosting border on a birthday cake.

"Very even," Angie said over her daughter's shoulder.

"Your turn." Sofie handed her mom the frosting bag for the more complicated flowers that would come next. Angie Ennemoser took the tool and squinted at the cake as though she could already see how it would end up. Her hair was in a braided bun with a hairnet made from golden threads. Her belief was that if she was going to wear a hairnet, it might as well be pretty. Sofie preferred a brown one that blended in with her hair.

She otherwise resembled her mom a great deal. They had the same shade of blue eyes and the same pouty lips. It annoyed Sofie when she was younger when people said they could be sisters. Though only in her twenties now, Sofie was already seeing the potential benefit of taking after a mom who looked young for her age.

Sofie's dad took a completely different approach to avoid the issue of hairnets altogether. He kept his head shaved.

"Oh, I forgot to tell you," Sofie said, "Amber's coming in this evening to place her order."

Ken Ennemoser smiled as he looked up from the large bowl of chocolate cake batter. His eyes peered over the top of his wire-rimmed glasses. "Are we supposed to pretend we haven't known of her affinity for carrot cake for years?"

"Just let her give us the details in person so she feels like a real bride. And she's bringing Joe."

"Yea!" Sofie's mom put down her frosting bag to clap excitedly. "I can't believe we haven't met him yet."

"You'll like him."

"I'm sure we will. Now stop distracting me." Angie Ennemoser picked up a different bag and began putting yellow centers in the flowers. She was the only true artist in the family. Sofie's dad had enough practice by now that he could decorate a cake beautifully, as long as he followed one of his wife's designs. Sofie planned to stick mostly to the business side of the business for a while and prayed she would have many years to learn from her mom before she had to do any cakes on her own.

Sofie was helping another customer when Amber and Joe entered the bakery only about fifteen minutes after five. She very politely pointed them to a table where they could wait as though Amber hadn't sat at that cute table sampling cake many times over the years. Her parents and Amber waved at each other – not as subtly as they thought – as the young couple took their seats. The middle-aged woman giving Sofie an order suppressed a smile at the interaction. She gave the last details and Sofie assured her that her cake would be ready on time.

As soon as the door closed on the other customer, Sofie dropped her professional demeanor and rushed over to her friends. Her parents must have rushed even more because they came from farther inside the shop and converged on the table the same time as Sofie.

"I can't believe you girls are big enough for us to be discussing an actual wedding cake," Angie said. "But first, introductions." She grinned and looked pointedly between Amber and Joe.

"Of course." Amber puffed herself up. "Mr. and Mrs. Ennemoser, a. k. a. Sofie's mom and dad, this is my future husband, Joe Hernandez."

"We're so happy to meet you." Angie beamed approvingly at Joe.

Sofie's dad thrust his hand out. "It's a pleasure, son. You can call us Ken and Angie if you're comfortable with that. Shall we get right to the tasting?"

"Okay, Ken," Joe said as he briefly shook the offered hand.

"We don't need to taste anything. We already know your cake is delicious."

"Nonsense." Angie waved her daughter towards the back to get the tray they'd prepared. "We're going to do this right."

When Sofie returned with the samples, her dad was giving Joe marriage advice. "Even when you don't really care, you need to have some say in the planning," he said, "otherwise, your wife is going to start the marriage thinking *she's* in charge when the man is supposed to be in charge. Right, honey?" He turned to his wife.

"That's right," she said. "The man is in charge whenever his wife gives him permission."

Sofie laughed only because of the number of times she'd heard the same routine. Customers were frequently subjected to it. It wasn't new to Amber either but her smile was not patronizing. Perhaps it sounded different as a bride.

The interest was evident on Joe's face when Sofie placed the sample tray on the table. "I think José will be happy to taste the cakes even if you don't need to," Sofie observed. Then she mentally kicked herself. She'd been trying to stop calling him José now that they were out of school.

He only nodded and kept his eyes on the desserts.

Amber grinned. "I didn't say I minded."

"All right," Angie said. "We just had to come over to say hello. We'll leave you kids to work out the details with Sofie. Pick whatever you like without looking at the cost though."

"That's right." Ken put one arm around his wife. "The cake will be our present to you."

"Wow, Mr. and Mrs. Ennemoser, that's really generous of you."

Joe's dark lashes lifted as he tore his eyes away from the treats to thank Sofie's parents.

Ken winked. "It's a gift for me, too," he said. "Makes shopping easy."

Joe laughed and Angie threw her elbow into her husband's side before she led him back to the kitchen half of the bakery.

"Dig in," Sofie said. "Then we can make your flavor choice official."

Sofie watched as they practiced for their wedding day by feeding each other the cake bites. She'd have thought they were an adorable couple even if they weren't such good friends. Joe pretended not to like the carrot cake they both knew was Amber's favorite. She shook back her thick mane of hair as she laughed at him. It was a beautiful golden brown and hung in waves around her shoulders. Sofie's hair was nearly identical in color but less shiny and she had half as much of it.

Joe almost put his hand in his own black hair before he noticed the frosting on his fingers and grabbed a napkin. Then he pushed the stray strands off his forehead.

Sofie filled out an order form with the expected preferences and the August wedding date that had been marked on her own calendar for months already. Joe and Amber stayed a few minutes after the details were recorded. Amber insisted that her parents wanted Sofie to come for dinner on Thursday. Sofie tried not to sound reluctant when she accepted, though she worried about who else might be invited.

2 PAST

S ofie Ennemoser clutched her books to her chest as she turned away from her locker. No one yelled, "Hi, new girl," as she made her way down the hall. She was glad that her novelty was wearing off. If she was merely one more body in the sea of students, no one would notice her detour. This was not the most direct path to her third period class. She'd come this way by mistake on the second day of school and couldn't resist the pull of this unnecessary extension in the days since.

She slowed her feet as the bottom of the stairwell came into view. After a few seconds, she saw him. Behind a girl who looked dangerously close to spilling the papers in her hands was a boy who looked – as usual – as though he'd never been introduced to a comb. He seemed completely unaware that anyone else was in the hall as he walked past Sofie and she began to follow him.

He was about a head taller than Sofie so she guessed he was in 7th or 8th grade – probably 8th – as she hadn't yet met a boy in her own grade who was taller than she was. A lock of brown hair was curling out to the side on the back of his head and she wished she could reach out and straighten it. She didn't even dare get that close. She simply followed until he entered the classroom she knew he would enter, the third one on the right. Then she rushed by with what she hoped was a subtle glance inside before she went around the corner to her English class.

Sofie took her seat at the desk by the wall. It was one of the last seats filled but still before the bell rang. The English teacher, Mrs. Dobbins, was sitting at a larger desk in a back corner of the room. She swept up to the front in a long, flowery skirt as soon as the bell rang. Only two weeks into the school year, Sofie had seen enough to expect more long, flowery skirts in the future.

Mrs. Dobbins had short hair in tight spirals that she was constantly trying to keep behind her ears. The spirals apparently had no intention of accepting that position.

"We have a fun project lined up for today, class," Mrs. Dobbins said, forcing back locks of hair that immediately popped out again. "You're going to work with a partner to make a small poster of…"

Sofie couldn't listen and count at the same time. She tallied her classmates and double-checked the number. It was evenly divisible by two. Sofie would likely have to work with the last person to get a partner, but at least she wouldn't be the leftover new girl who was assigned to an existing pair. She tuned back to Mrs. Dobbins' voice.

"…so the letters in the word verb will each represent actions and adjective will, I think, be the most fun. These are the words you'll need to include on your poster." She gestured to a list on the board. "Go ahead and pair up."

There was no one on Sofie's right so she looked to the girl on her left, who was already nodding to the girl on her left. Sofie turned to the girl behind her. "Do you have a partner?" she asked.

"I'm working with Jess."

Sofie nodded, though she didn't know who Jess was. If the next person she asked turned out to be Jess, she was going to look pretty stupid. Sofie was about to tap the boy in front of her on the shoulder when he waved to a boy two rows over who was waving back. Her options were shrinking by the moment. Sofie looked around the room with rising concern. Had she counted wrong?

"All right, settle down," Mrs. Dobbins said. She was holding a stack of colored cardstock with one hand and using the other to fight with her hair. "Does anyone still need a partner?"

Sofie raised her hand and looked around the room. A very red-faced girl in the back row also had her hand up.

Mrs. Dobbins pointed at her and then at Sofie. "Amber, you'll work with Sofie. Rearrange so you're sitting by your partners and then I'll pass out the paper." The teacher inhaled a calming breath as she appeared to regret giving the green light for pandemonium, even if it was only temporary.

Someone from the front zipped past Sofie and a boy sitting next to Amber jumped out of his seat so Sofie hurried to take his place. "Hi," she said to Amber, hoping she wasn't too upset with the partner assignment.

Amber had a long ponytail that was twisted rather than braided and it began to swing as she nodded a shy greeting.

Mrs. Dobbins walked up and down the rows asking the pairs which color of the stiff paper they wanted.

"What color do we want?" Sofie asked.

Her new partner pressed her lips together then hesitantly said, "Purple?"

"Perfect." Purple was Sofie's favorite color and she asked Mrs. Dobbins for it when she came to them.

"This project won't be due until Friday, but I'm only giving you class time today to work on it," the teacher said as she returned to the front of the room, "so if it doesn't look like you'll be finished before the bell, you'll need to take turns working on it or plan a time to meet during lunch or after school. But do try to have some fun with it." Mrs. Dobbins shoved some spirals behind her ear and moved towards her desk carrying leftover paper.

Sofie turned to Amber, who had copied the list of words from the board and was still staring at her notebook. It was probably time for Sofie to admit she hadn't paid enough attention to fully understand the project. "Um, so we have to draw each letter as an example of that type of word?"

Amber nodded, her thick ponytail swinging.

"Okay. Verb is first on the list." Sofie copied that one into her own notebook. "Can we make the V jumping?"

Very quietly, Amber said, "It has to start with V."

"Oh!" Sofie was kicking herself for not listening better to the instructions. Amber was probably wishing she had a different partner already. "How about…" She stared blankly at the paper for a minute.

Amber whispered something Sofie didn't hear.

"What?" she asked.

"Venting," she said a little louder.

Sofie considered the word. "That's good," she said. "We could draw the V open a little wider with squiggly lines coming out like it's venting something."

Behind the smile Amber was trying to hide, it seemed as though she wanted to say something. Sofie looked at her patiently.

"Should we... um... should we write out all the words first before we put them on the poster?"

"Good idea." Sofie wrote venting in her notebook and drew a V the way she had described. Amber did the same in her notebook.

"How about eats next?" Sofie suggested.

Amber nodded and began to write. Her E looked as though it was eating something while Sofie's E simply looked ill. Sofie would enjoy having help on the project. Though they seemed to be making good progress on words, their poster was still blank when Mrs. Dobbins announced to the class that they had only a few minutes left. They needed to arrange more time to work.

"Which lunch period do you have?" Sofie asked.

"First."

"Drat. I eat second. What days are you busy after school? It might be better if I go to your house because my parents are trying to open a bakery and I usually have to go there for a while after school and there wouldn't be any markers or... we'd have to bring any supplies we wanted to use."

Amber nodded as though she understood but was thoroughly overwhelmed by everything Sofie had just said. After a minute, Sofie managed to extract the number of the bus Amber rode home and an address for Sofie's mom to pick her up later. Then she asked for a last name and phone number because her mom might want to know that, too.

"Thanks. See you tomorrow." Sofie grabbed her books as the bell rang then plunged into the hallway. She discovered later that her farewell was inaccurate because Amber was also in her history class in the afternoon. They shared a smile as Sofie acknowledged her mistake.

Because her mom picked her up to take her to the almost bakery, Sofie was unfamiliar with the afternoon bus routine. She stuck close to Amber the next day, who seemed a bit bolder outside the classroom. They stood in the hallway watching a TV monitor not saying much until Amber pointed out her bus. Sofie followed her outside and up the steps of the third bus in line.

The driver greeted Amber by name in a very deep voice and then looked immediately to Sofie's hand. She was holding out the pass she'd gotten from the office. "Welcome aboard," he said, his voice friendly but also loud and booming.

Sofie took the seat next to Amber in the front row before she thought of a potential problem. "Does someone else usually sit here?"

Amber shook her head and lowered her eyes to the floor.

Sofie looked past her to the kids still on the sidewalk. It didn't appear the bus would be very full. She glanced up at the kid turning into the aisle and was startled by a familiar face. The boy from the hallway rode this bus. Sofie wanted to watch to see how far back he sat but was afraid someone would guess her interest. She locked her eyes on the seat in front of her. There was a small tear in the green fabric near the seam.

"My stop is second," Amber's voice said from next to her.

Sofie continued to stare at the foam beneath the green. She worked to dislodge her attention from its real focus and nodded at Amber's information.

At the first stop, only two kids got off. They were both girls. Sofie stood at the second stop and walked straight off the bus in front of Amber. She wanted to look back, wanted to know if a certain person was also getting off, but her head simply refused to turn that way.

The bus stop was a corner and Amber gestured to the right. Sofie fell into step next to her and was vaguely aware that other kids had gotten off and that most of them seemed to be going straight instead. Sofie had almost convinced her head to look at those kids when a boy with longer legs and a quicker pace passed Amber on her other side. Amber acted as though she didn't even notice him.

Sofie tried to act as though she, too, was unconcerned by his presence. "So… uh… what did your parents say about me coming over?"

"They're fine with it," Amber said. "Although they won't actually be there. At least not at first. My mom will get home before your mom comes to pick you up. This is the first year they let us come home before they get off work. Last year we had to go to our grandparents' house." Amber smiled shyly. She looked proud.

But there was something bugging Sofie about what she'd just said. Who was us and who was we?

"Don't get me wrong," Amber quickly added. "I like my grandparents. It'd just be embarrassing to still have a babysitter. My brother will be home though."

Amber threw out that last sentence like an unimportant afterthought. Sofie was afraid it might be very, very important. She was looking ahead to the tall boy with messed up hair and jeans as he turned and suddenly sprinted up the sidewalk to a yellow house on his left. What were the odds that Amber's brother was already in a different house or... behind them?

Sofie's head worked just fine as she checked the sidewalk trailing them. There was one more kid from the bus. A girl. Amber's brother must be in a different house. He couldn't be...

But he was. Amber turned up the same sidewalk. She led Sofie up to the same door. She tried to turn the handle and sighed. Then she rolled her eyes while she took off her backpack and said, "Austin thinks it's funny to lock me out when I'm right behind him. Fortunately, we both have keys." She pulled a rabbit's foot with a key dangling from it out of a zippered pocket on her backpack.

Amber pushed the door open and Sofie followed her inside while her mind buzzed with questions about what might happen. His name was Austin, and he was somewhere in this house.

Amber led the way to the kitchen without saying anything. She tossed her backpack onto the table and began to unzip it. Sofie stood stiffly nearby waiting, though she didn't know for what.

"I have the purple poster," Amber said, "and we can use my notes." She didn't whisper in her own home.

Sofie nodded, exhaled slowly, and took a seat next to Amber. Their project was their focus for a while. Sofie forgot to be tense as she colored the letter pictures Amber drew. They worked too well together as they quickly moved on to doodling letters they didn't need for the project. The poster sat only half-finished while they flipped to a third page in Amber's notebook.

A loud thump startled Sofie and interrupted their laughter. Someone had just jumped to the floor from about halfway up the stairs. He came into the kitchen, looked right at Sofie and said, "Who are you?"

He had deep blue eyes in the middle of an otherwise pale face. They poured heat into her body and drilled a hole in her brain through which all intelligent thought leaked out. Instead of her name she said, "Hi."

"You can just ignore him," Amber said at the same time.

Austin shrugged and walked past them. Sofie heard a refrigerator open behind her. She heard a cupboard bang shut and was even aware of the vibrations of heavy footsteps around the room. Ignoring the presence of Amber's brother did not feel like a viable option. Sofie trained her eyes on the growling G Amber was drawing, though it was less amusing than it had been a moment ago.

Austin returned to the table. He set a glass of what looked like grape juice on the corner and asked, "What are you working on?"

Amber shrieked and picked up the purple cardstock. "Don't put that there," she said. "If you spill it, our homework will be ruined."

"Relax. I'm not a toddler." Austin rolled his eyes at his sister and repeated, "What are you working on?"

Amber said nothing. She glared at her brother while she set the project back on the table on the corner farthest from his glass.

"You gonna tell me?"

"Why do you want to know?" she asked.

"It's called curiosity."

"It's called none of your business."

Sofie wanted to answer Austin's question, but she worried about getting between them. She had no siblings. Would Amber be mad if she spoke up or was she only enjoying giving her brother a hard time? "It's for English," Sofie said, hoping a half-answer would be helpful enough for the sibling she wanted to impress and not too helpful for the sibling she wanted to call her friend.

Amber didn't seem to care that she had said anything. Austin had been looking at the table during the sparring and didn't need help. "Oh," he said, "you guys have Mrs. Dobbins, don't you?"

"You already know that," Amber said.

"I remember this letter thing." Austin picked up his glass, took a long drink, then set it on a nearby counter. "She had them hanging around the room the rest of the year so I hope you like looking at them."

"It's better than looking at *you*. Right, Sofie?"

They both looked at her and Sofie wished right down to her toes, right down to the littlest toenail on her littlest toe, that they hadn't stopped ignoring her. She felt it couldn't be any more obvious that she'd been gawking at Austin than if she shouted the fact. But even now that he noticed her again, there was no spark of recognition, no hint at all that he remembered helping her.

He was the one who had stopped. That first time she passed him in the hall, the time she'd been there by mistake, she called out a general plea for information and Austin explained her wrong turn while other kids laughed at the poor lost 6th grader. Even knowing the incident was thoroughly elevated and romanticized in her own memory, it still rankled Sofie to see that it had left no impression whatsoever on Austin. Yet at the same time, she began to hope her current befuddlement would prove equally forgettable.

"Uh... what?" Sofie turned to Amber as though she didn't understand the question.

"Sorry." Amber smiled and lifted one shoulder. "Putting up with him all the time is exhausting. Sometimes I run out of good insults."

Austin picked up his drink and left the room. They could hear him laughing as he went back upstairs.

"Maybe we should go to my room to finish this. Just in case he comes back," Amber said.

Sofie didn't argue. A clock on the wall caught her attention as she boxed up the colored pencils and glitter markers they'd been using. "Oh, look at the time," she said. "I think my mom will be here before we're done."

Amber looked at their progress and at the clock. "I guess we got a bit distracted." Her expression was guilty, but Sofie smiled. She'd been having fun.

"Maybe... um..." Sofie was more hesitant about inviting herself over a second time. But school work was important. School work might make it less impolite. "Maybe I could come over another day?"

The guilt dissolved from Amber's face. "Tomorrow?" she suggested hopefully.

Sofie nodded and finished putting away the supplies. Amber moved the project to what she said would be a safe place. Now that they had plotted to get together again, doing homework seemed unnecessary. Sofie told Amber a little about the work of opening a bakery, and Amber asked where she had moved from.

"Do you miss your old school?"

"Not really." Sofie shrugged. "I'd have started a new school this year anyway, and I didn't leave any close friends. Plus here no one – at least so far – no one calls me..."

"Calls you what?"

Amber appeared sympathetic before she even heard the dreaded nickname. Surely she could be trusted not to spread it around. But Sofie really hated it and that made her cautious. "Promise you won't tell anyone?"

"I promise."

"At my old school... people called me... they called me Eenie-meenie-miney-moser."

Amber laughed but quickly put her hand over her mouth. "Sorry," she said. "I know that wouldn't be funny at school."

At school, it wouldn't be funny. But here, in Amber's safe kitchen, Sofie could almost see the humor herself. Almost.

"Mom's home," Austin's voice announced.

Sofie jumped at how close it seemed while Amber didn't even acknowledge the sound.

Sofie turned nervously towards the voice and saw Austin standing at the top of the stairs. He was looking right at her. Had he heard the nickname, too? More importantly, did he think it was funny?

3 PRESENT

Austin was flipping through the pages of a sports magazine – and bothering no one – when his sister sat down across from him at the table. He paused on the current page, though his eyes weren't picking up anything particularly interesting.

Amber placed her hands palms down on the table between them and began to wiggle her fingers just past the top of the magazine. The movement invaded his peripheral vision. He sucked the edge of his bottom lip against his teeth to avoid smiling. He calmly turned a page.

She curled her fingers so that they wiggled and tapped on the table at the same time. Austin couldn't pretend to read the full page advertisement so he turned to the next page. Baseball stats. His eyes ran down the first column, but it was difficult to concentrate on the numbers with Amber's fingernails clicking against the wood. When she loudly cleared her throat, he decided he had annoyed her long enough. He tried to look up as though he'd just noticed her. "Do you need something?"

She rolled her eyes, not buying his innocent act. "Do you like Sofie?"

"Sofie Ennemoser?"

She rolled her eyes again. Apparently, she didn't buy the dumb act either. "Yes. What other Sofie do we know?"

"Didn't Rob marry someone named Sofie?" Rob was their cousin. He was completely irrelevant to the conversation and Austin knew that.

"It was Sofia," Amber corrected. "But who cares?"

"You asked me if we knew any other Sofies."

Amber sighed so heavily he could feel her breath on his hands. "Just answer my question."

"I did. We know the Sofie that Rob married."

"*Sofia*. And not that question."

If she could hide her frustration better, Amber would be so much less fun to tease. Austin would still refuse to tell her exactly what she wanted to know. It was a question he needed to explore with Sofie first. He was, however, beginning to think that it was not his imagination that Sofie was avoiding him. She couldn't possibly still be mad though. It had been a year. "Look," he said, "you two have been friends forever. I think you'd know by now if I had a problem with Sofie."

"I didn't ask if you had a problem with her."

"You wanted to know if I didn't like her."

"No. I asked if you *liked* her and you know that's not the same thing."

"Do I?"

Amber stared back and instead of getting more frustrated, she let out a short laugh. "Oh, you're not fooling me," she said. "You're being difficult because you don't want to answer the question. I think that means you have something to hide."

"If you want to think that, I can't stop you." Austin tried to appear unconcerned as he turned his attention back to the magazine. Yes, he definitely wanted to date Sofie. But there was no way he was going to admit anything to Amber, no way he was going to let her think she was involved. He needed to talk to Sofie quickly, before Amber got any ideas about playing match-maker.

Something in the kitchen began to beep and Amber left him alone to silence it. "Mom," she called out, "should I take the ham out of the oven?"

Their mom, Charlene Waits, drifted into the kitchen and pulled open the oven door. Austin stared at the short curls on her head. Only a few days ago, she had decided that gray roots would be easier to hide with a lighter color and she dyed her hair blond. Austin had known her with brown hair for twenty-four years and thought it might take him that long to get used to the new shade. At least he had enough sense not to tell her she looked weird. "Ten more minutes," she said about the meat. Then she looked at Austin. "You staying for dinner, honey?"

He nodded.

Amber scoffed. "That's the whole reason he's here." She reset the timer and walked back to the table. She did not sit. "You're like a stray dog, you know. Just wandering over for meals."

"I live close," he said. "And Mom is a wonderful cook."

His mom cast her eyes towards the ceiling at the blatant flattery and looked amused by it.

Amber leaned across the table as though she was about to share a secret, but she didn't lower her voice. "I don't mind that you're staying this time because Sofie is coming over. I'm going to be watching you."

The doorbell rang as Amber finished her threat. "Maybe that's her now." She raced towards the door.

Austin's mom took his sister's place in front of him. "Are you and Sofie having some sort of problem?" she asked. The concern on her face mixed with something that looked oddly like hope.

"No," Austin said. "Amber is just trying to cause one."

Charlene Waits followed her daughter to greet the visitor. Austin stayed where he was. He could already hear that it was Joe. Sofie arrived a minute later. Then Austin and Amber's father, Doug Waits, descended the stairs and observed that there were an awful lot of people in his kitchen and not nearly enough of them setting the table for dinner. He was mostly joking, but Austin took the hint to put away the magazine and get out a stack of plates.

Sofie made a move for the nearby silverware drawer but kept her eyes carefully focused on the utensils.

"Hi, Sofie," Austin said.

"Hi." She smiled before she whirled away from him with a handful of forks. "Mrs. Waits," she said, "Amber told me you dyed your hair. It looks great."

"Thank you." Her hand came up to pat the side of her head. "I'm glad you like it. Austin thinks I look weird."

Several heads turned accusingly in Austin's direction. He was positive he'd never said that out loud so he had no qualms about denying it. "I did not say that."

"You didn't have to," she said. "But don't worry, honey. I know you'll get used to it." His mom smiled and motioned him towards the table with the plates, or perhaps out of the way of the oven.

Amber and Joe brought over glasses. Amber was the only one of the younger generation living in the house, but they'd all eaten there enough to know where things were kept.

Austin mostly ate and listened during dinner. The food was delicious and the chatter not too boring. Sofie entertained them all with a story about a very indecisive customer. And Amber didn't mention her upcoming wedding even once.

Sofie was sitting next to Austin and she smelled like the inside of the bakery. That kind of made him hope she brought dessert. She also looked beautiful. Her eyes seemed to dance as she talked about the customer trying to decide if she wanted her anniversary sentiments spelled out in print letters or script. That more than kind of made him hope to have better luck getting her alone tonight.

They'd had dinner with his family together twice since she came home from school. Both times he thought he could walk her out. The first time, she snuck out while he was in the bathroom. The second, she appeared to get a phone call as she was leaving. Austin didn't like suspecting her of faking the call. He liked even less the look of anxiety she'd thrown his way as she reached for the phone. Perhaps tonight she'd be ready to talk.

Once dinner was over and the kitchen cleaned up, everyone gathered in the family room for some chitchat. Six people pretty much filled the room and all the available seats. Amber was between Sofie and Joe on the larger sofa, though she was closer to Joe. Austin got a fat-armed chair to himself and his parents took the striped loveseat.

"I think we've built enough anticipation," Charlene said. She looked at Amber. "When do we get to shop for the dress?"

Wedding talk. Austin half-listened as Amber tried to describe the dress she had in mind with hand gestures and words that didn't explain anything to him. He didn't bother to ask for clarification. He watched Sofie nodding at the description. After a minute, she looked in his direction. She smiled when their eyes met but quickly looked away. She appeared to have less control of her mouth because it kept trying to smile. Her eyes fought her, too. He could tell she was trying not to look, but they kept finding him, kept casting glances to see if he was still looking at her. Austin could watch all day. She was fascinating. Hard to figure out at times but always fascinating.

Sofie's voice suddenly broke into the monotony of bodice and fabric descriptions. "I think we're boring the guys," she said.

Austin nodded at her. She clearly pretended not to see it. But Amber noticed. "No one cares if you're bored, Austin. You can go home," she said. "But we can talk about something else if Joe is bored." She looked to her future husband.

Sofie leaned around her. "Go ahead, José." Her voice carried a taunt. "Tell her how you're tired of talking about your wedding."

"Don't try to get Joe in trouble," Doug Waits said. "I can admit I'm bored and I live here." He flashed Austin a commiserating wink.

Joe could take care of himself though. He said, "I'm afraid the details are lost on me but only because I know Amber will look beautiful in any dress."

"Thank you." Amber smiled sappily.

While his sister was appeased, Austin was irritated by the exchange. He did not like that Sofie seemed to have an inside joke with another guy, even if that guy was about to marry someone else. It was time to get to the bottom of the name business. "Why do you call him José when no one else does?" He looked at Joe. "Joe is short for Joseph, right?"

Joe nodded.

"I never meant for it to become a habit," Sofie said. She leaned forward again to look at Joe. "I can try harder to stop if it bothers you."

"I don't mind. I got the much better end of the deal." He took hold of Amber's hand and squeezed it while he smiled at her.

"Aww!" Austin's mom sounded like a litter of puppies had just paraded into the room. "Now I need to hear the story."

"Didn't Amber tell you all how they met through me?" Sofie was looking around the room but mostly at the Amber's parents.

"She only told us they met at school." Charlene gave her daughter a look of indignation.

"Do you want to tell it?" Sofie asked her couch mates.

Joe shook his head and Amber said, "The floor is yours."

Austin interrupted before Sofie could start. "I thought you were going to tell us why you call him José."

"It's the same story."

"How is—?"

"If you let her tell it, you'll know," Amber cut in.

Austin put his hands up in surrender. He hadn't even been trying to annoy her that time. He sat back and waited for Sofie.

"Okay," she said. "Joe and I had a class together the second semester of our first year. We sat next to each other and were a little friendly. It was a class on international business and one day there was a picture in the book of a sign that was in Spanish. I asked Joe, because he was sitting next to me, if he had any idea what it said and he could only read part of it. He thanked me for not looking shocked at that. Then he explained that it alternated between annoying and embarrassing when people came up to him speaking Spanish because they assumed based on his appearance that he would understand."

Though Joe's grandparents were from Mexico, both his mom and his dad were born in the US and were more fluent in English than Spanish. Joe learned even less Spanish than his parents.

"So that same day," Sofie continued, "as we were about to leave class, another guy came up and asked, um, Joe about something. Clarification on the pages we were supposed to read for homework, I think. Then he said, 'Thanks, José.' And Joe said, 'You're welcome. But my name is Joe.' And the other guy said, 'Really? I thought the prof was just Americanizing it for you.' Joe just said, 'It's Joe.'"

Sofie paused for a moment while everyone in the room appreciated her half-annoyed, half-confused impression of Joe. "I asked him if that sort of thing happened a lot, too. He said,

'No. That was a first.' So I called him José the next couple of classes to kid around and that would have been the end of it except…"

Sofie took a deep, dramatic breath and waved her hand towards Amber. "This is where Amber comes in. She had a class at the same time in the building right next door so we would meet up outside and walk home together. Joe noticed this, or rather he noticed Amber, because he asked me about her. It was obvious why he was asking so I said he should walk out with me so I could make some introductions. But I also made a threat. I said if he started monopolizing my friend's time so I couldn't see her as much, then I was going to keep calling him José as revenge. And you know what he said to that?"

Sofie directed the question to Amber's mom, who saw Amber grinning and leaned closer. "What did he say?" she asked.

"He said, 'If she lets me monopolize her time, you can call me anything you want.'"

"How sweet." Charlene Waits clearly approved of the answer.

Amber was still wearing an absurd grin.

Austin might have been tempted to roll his eyes except that he was growing increasingly desperate for just a few minutes of Sofie's time. What price would he pay?

"I really never meant for it to become a habit though," Sofie repeated. "I called him José the first few times he came to pick her up and before I knew it I couldn't stop. But I know it's childish. I'm trying to stop before the wedding."

"Know what else you need to do before the wedding?"

Sofie eyed Amber warily, as though she expected a list.

"You have to help me address forty-seven envelopes."

"Forty-seven?" Sofie asked. "Are you sure that's final this time?"

"It better be. We need to send them out pretty soon. Oh!" Amber sat up straighter as though she'd just been poked with something sharp. "But I did change my mind about the flowers."

"I'm glad you talked me out of ordering them then," Charlene said.

Amber stood and grabbed Sofie's hand to pull her from the couch. "Come upstairs," she said. "I want to show you some pictures."

"I need to see, too." Charlene followed the other women from the room with a giddy smile.

Doug Waits clapped his hands and began rubbing them together. "They're going to be a while," he said. "Who's up for croquet? It's excellent croquet weather today."

"I'm in," Austin said. He looked at Joe. "You remember how to play?"

"Yes. Your dad even loaned me a few books on the subject."

"I'm not surprised," Austin said.

"I'll be nice and give you a few weeks before I ask if you've read them." It wasn't clear if Doug Waits was kidding his future son-in-law or not. He had a bizarre obsession with croquet. Austin thought that if his dad was in the mood for a game, even a hurricane would be considered excellent croquet weather. Joe sighed as he moved from the family room, likely thinking that he should read a few chapters just in case.

The wickets were already set up in the backyard. Austin narrowly defeated his dad and Joe held his own surprisingly well for a novice. His dad suggested they play another game right away so Joe could keep practicing. Joe was up for it, but Austin returned to the house. When he got inside, his mom and his sister were sitting at the table looking at wedding invitations. As far as he could tell, they weren't trying to address them or stick them in envelopes or anything useful. They were simply looking at them.

He glanced around the kitchen.

"Sofie went home," Amber said.

"Okay." Austin tried to acknowledge his sister without giving her the satisfaction of knowing she'd answered the question he hadn't asked.

"I tried to get her to wait for your game to end. She said Dad was probably going to talk you guys into playing all night." Amber shrugged helplessly. "There really was no way to argue with that."

Austin agreed. Silently. In words he only told them he was going to head home as well. If this had been the first time he missed leaving with Sofie, he'd have had no cause to think her reasoning was suspicious. Now it only seemed convenient.

4 PAST

"How about croquet?" Dillon said. He pointed to a box on the back steps.

Austin grimaced at his friend. "No way. My dad has been relentless lately. I think I played with him ten times this weekend."

Dillon had red hair that looked more fiery than usual in the bright sunshine. He stuck one hand in it while he tried to think of something else they might do.

A suggestion came from over the fence instead. "Austin! Wanna play?"

There were three boys next door, ages seven, ten and eleven. The oldest one, Levi, was peering over the fence with a soccer ball held in the air. They'd been asking Austin over a lot this summer to even up their teams. But with Dillon, they'd be odd again. Austin pointed to his friend and spoke to Levi. "We'd have five today."

"Will your sister play?" Dillon asked. He sounded hopeful and on board with the neighbor kids' suggestion.

Amber was unlikely to play though. She didn't like soccer. But she had a friend over. "I bet I can get Sofie to play," Austin said. "I'll be right back."

Dillon went through the gate to the next yard while Austin slid open the door and walked into his house. He spotted Sofie and Amber immediately. They were on the family room floor sorting through a pile of beads. "Hey," he said, "we need one more for soccer."

Amber shook her head quickly and scrunched up her nose. Sofie looked at Amber and then shook her head without looking up.

"Come on," Austin said. "One of you has to play."

"Not me," Amber said.

Sofie bit the side of her lip like she was thinking about it.

"Come on," Austin said again. "Who's it gonna be?" He held up his hand to point at them. "Eenie… meenie…"

Sofie jumped to her feet. "Fine," she said. "I'll play."

Austin grinned. It was way too easy. Sofie would agree to almost anything if he threatened to tell anyone what she hated to be called. The funny thing was that he was sure she could tell it was an empty threat, even more so now that he was about to move on to high school.

"Wait for me," Amber said as she began to follow them.

"You can't both play," Austin protested. "That defeats the purpose of evening the teams."

Amber stuck her hands on her hips. "You can't stop me. But I don't want to play anyway. I'm going to *watch*."

"Are they both playing?" Dillon asked as Austin escorted the girls into the neighbors' yard.

Austin gestured to the one who was not his sister. "Just Sofie."

Dillon nodded and looked over the players. "You and I should probably be on opposite teams."

That sounded fair to Austin since they were the two oldest. When he played with the three neighbor boys, he was always paired with the middle brother who no one would say out loud was the weakest player. No one admitted the tiny 7-year-old was the best goalie either. Getting anything past the blond ball of energy was tough. He guarded that net like his life depended on it. Dillon would think Austin was being generous – at least at first – to put the youngest on his team. He pointed at the little guy and said, "I'll take Devin."

"Because Sofie is a *girl?*" Amber inserted herself into the team choosing out of nowhere, finding offense from less just because Austin was involved.

"I thought you were only watching," he said.

"I am."

"Watch quieter."

She scowled while a few of the guys chuckled.

"Devin, you want to be with me?"

Devin nodded vigorously and jumped in front of a goal without waiting for any discussion about who would play that position.

"I'll take Levi," Dillon said.

"Sofie is good." Amber looked between Dillon and Austin defiantly. "One of you is going to be so sorry you didn't want the girl on your team."

"Yeah, that's what I said." Austin put up a sarcasm shield. He was trying to pretend Amber wasn't even watching. He might have asked Sofie to join his team next, but not if Amber was going to make a challenge out of it. He waved the other brother over to join him and Devin.

Sofie didn't seem to care whose team she was on as she talked with Dillon and Levi. They decided to let Levi goaltend first for their team.

Amber folded her arms and her legs as she took a seat on the steps of the deck. It didn't take long for half of her prediction to come true. Though it didn't have anything to do with whether or not she was a girl, Austin *was* sorry she wasn't on his team. She was good. Probably better than he was. His team was ahead four to two, but only because Devin was on fire. Sofie had scored both goals for the other team and the second time she'd stolen the ball from Austin to do it. Then she scored again.

With the score still close, the ball came loose on the opposing side of the field. Austin ran for it and so did Sofie. He sensed that a wild shot towards the goal would be better than letting Sofie get anywhere near it. They arrived at it together and rather than meeting the ball, Austin's foot connected with Sofie's shin.

"Ow!" she screamed and hit the ground.

Levi grabbed the ball and ran up to see if Sofie was all right. Everyone else gathered around as well. Sofie was sitting in the grass with both hands holding her leg and saying, "I'm fine. I'm fine. I'm fine." The pain was so evident on her face that she might have been trying to convince herself.

Austin knew he was responsible, even if it had been an accident, so he wanted to help. He bent down to pick her up. "I'll take you inside and let my mom put ice on it."

"No!" Sofie let go of her leg and used her hands to slide herself backwards, away from his hands. She stared up at him with wide eyes that glistened with the tears she was refusing to let fall. "I'm fine," she said again.

It occurred to Austin that his sister's friend was actually a very pretty girl and that carrying her might be… a lot different than carrying his sister. He couldn't fully appreciate even the thought before Sofie scrambled to her feet. "Let's keep playing," she said.

Austin looked down and saw a bruise beginning to appear on her shin. But the other guys were getting back into position and if she didn't want to stop, she'd probably get mad if he tried to make her. She favored that leg the rest of the game though and was less aggressive, particularly if Austin was nearby. He had the weirdest feeling that she wasn't afraid of him, but rather was afraid he would feel bad if he hurt her again.

Though he was distracted, Austin's team still managed a close victory. Dillon wasn't exactly gracious. "We'd have won," he said, "if Austin hadn't hobbled one of our players."

Austin said, "It was an accident."

Sofie said the same thing at the same time. Then she bit back a smile and rushed towards Amber.

"It's still the only reason you won," Dillon insisted. "We'll get you next time but I gotta get home now. My mom will be mad if I'm late for dinner." He waved and started jogging as soon as he left the yard. He lived right around the corner.

Austin said goodbye to Levi and his brothers before he followed Amber and Sofie home. They only entered the house a minute before him, but it was enough time for his mom to spot the black and blue and puffy mark on Sofie's leg. She must have asked what happened because as Austin came through the door, he heard Sofie say, "We were playing soccer," while Amber said, "Austin kicked her."

Charlene Waits might have hurt herself if she had whipped her head around any faster to check Austin's reaction to this accusation.

"It was an accident," he said. Sofie's voice matched his again. He tried to share a smile with her, but she had turned her back to him.

His mom was still giving him a sharp look. "I hope you at least apologized."

"He didn't," Amber said too quickly.

"Sit down, Sofie." Austin's mom directed her to a chair. "I'm going to give you some ice."

"You don't have to. It really doesn't hurt that much."

"It's swollen." She opened the freezer and pulled out a blue pouch. "I'm going to feel terrible if your mom comes to get you and I have to tell her I didn't do anything for it."

Sofie sat somewhat reluctantly and held the ice pack to her leg. She shifted in the chair so that she was practically facing the corner.

As much as it pained Austin to admit his sister was right about anything, he had forgotten something important. He tried to get Sofie's attention just by moving a little closer. He would have preferred to mouth a private apology but when Sofie continued to concentrate on the ice, he had to say it out loud. "I'm sorry you got hurt, Sofie."

She nodded that she'd heard but still didn't look up. Amber, however, stared at him like he'd just said it in Parseltongue.

"Oh, Amber?"

"Yes?" She answered her mom without taking her incredulous eyes off Austin.

"Sarah Stone called for you while you were outside."

"Again?" Amber huffed and sat next to Sofie. They shared a sympathizing look.

"Is there a reason you can't be friendly towards this Sarah?" Her mom's tone had a hint of warning in it.

"I try, Mom," Amber said. "But she's only trying to get me to invite her over here because she likes Austin."

That sounded like Austin's cue to leave the room. He planned to disappear subtly by moving first to the sink for some water and then out the other side of the kitchen.

His mom looked amused. "Amber," she said, "you might have to accept the fact that Austin might someday date one of your friends."

"Eww, Mom. There's no way that's ever going to happen."

Austin should have finished his exit by that point. But since he hadn't, he said, "I don't think you have anything to worry about since you don't have any friends."

Amber didn't respond to him. She looked at Sofie instead. "I keep telling you my brother is an idiot. He can't even count to one."

Sofie laughed but kept her eyes on the ice pack she didn't want on the injury Austin had inflicted. He was still pretty sure that Amber didn't have anything to worry about.

5 PRESENT

S he was a wonderful person. Austin truly loved his grandmother. He felt bad about needing to remind himself that she was a wonderful person as they walked out of the church together. Sofie had switched to attending the early mass. Two could play that game. Austin got up early for church, intending to find Sofie and sit with her. Even if they couldn't talk much, he could at least be near her.

His grandmother unknowingly foiled his plan. She spotted him before he could spot Sofie and insisted he take the empty place next to her. She made her way slowly towards the back afterwards. Her cane made a thump and a squeak with every step. Austin normally had plenty of patience for the kind woman, even with her attempts to marry him off to every woman she met, but today he was trying to catch Sofie.

She left the church ahead of them but wasn't rushing to the parking lot. He could see her standing on the sidewalk just outside the open door, her hair and yellow skirt blowing in what must be a very warm breeze. It looked as though she was waiting for someone. Her back was to Austin but maybe she'd seen him inside. Maybe she would let him broach the subject he wanted to broach. Maybe this time she wouldn't run away.

"Slow down, Austin. These short legs couldn't keep up with you even if my balance was what it used to be."

"Sorry, Gran." And he was sorry. Now that she had his attention, Austin could hear her labored breathing and see the way she was struggling with her cane. If he couldn't talk to Sofie today, he'd just keep trying. He made a deliberate effort to match his grandmother's pace and held his arm out to her.

She smiled up at him as she took hold. "I hope you're in a hurry to meet my young friend."

"Alexa, right? You know I'm only going to say hello."

"That's all I'm asking," she said. There was artificial innocence in her voice. That was all she was asking today. The woman was not shy about expressing her belief that Austin needed to "settle down with a nice girl." Sooner rather than later. Fortunately, she had also pointed out on numerous occasions that Sofie was a nice girl. Austin believed he had a fair shot at making his grandmother happy... eventually.

She nodded her head towards the exit Austin had been trying not to fixate on. "Isn't that Amber?"

Austin saw her, too. Amber had just appeared on the sidewalk next to Sofie. They both laughed at whatever Amber said as a greeting and began walking to the left, the direction of the parish hall. They must be heading for coffee. "I don't think she noticed us," Austin said.

"No. Too busy with her friend. Isn't Sofie the girl you took to your prom?"

He nodded.

"She's a nice girl."

"She is."

"Then why haven't you married her?"

He tried not to laugh because he knew she was serious. "There's no beating around the bush with you, is there, Gran?"

"But there is with you," she returned his smile with sharp eyes, "because you didn't answer my question."

"The thing is... I can't marry someone without her permission."

"And you can't get permission if you don't ask for it."

"Point taken," he said.

She looked as though she doubted that, as though she was considering how else to impress upon him the importance of holy matrimony. If she had any other comments on the topic, she kept them for a later round. She said nothing else except a few complaints about the summer heat before they made it to the hall.

There were dozens of people already inside the hall, most of them already enjoying coffee and/or donuts. Amber and Sofie were sitting alone at a table on the far end of the room. Austin waved to them. Amber scrunched her face at him and then smiled at their grandmother while cradling a paper cup between her hands. He and his grandmother received the same warm smile from Sofie. It seemed she had no problem looking happy to see him when there were witnesses.

"She is a nice girl."

"I know, Gran. Shall I get you a donut?"

"Just coffee for me, thank you."

Austin nodded and picked up a donut for himself before he filled a cup for his grandmother. She led him to what she said was her usual table and dropped her cane against the side of it while Austin helped her with her chair. "Hello, ladies," she said to the two women seated there. One of them appeared close to his grandmother's age, though he might have been wrong because he was trying to guess her age through a thick coat of make-up. The dark-haired woman was decades younger.

The metal folding chair creaked as his grandmother lowered herself and looked up at Austin. "Austin, honey, I want you to meet some of my friends. That's Suzy and this here is Alexa."

The older woman looked at him like a hungry piranha and the younger woman simply looked wary. Austin was glad his grandmother hadn't tried to get him to stick around. "Hi," he said. "It's nice to meet both of you. I'm sorry I can't stay."

Alexa visibly relaxed at the news that he wasn't staying. "Glad to finally put a face with the name," she said. "Your grandmother is a fan."

"I'm sure she is." Austin returned the smile of the young woman who was evidently more amused by the match-making effort than interested in it. "Hope you enjoy your coffee, Gran."

Austin took a bite of donut with one hand and waved with the other as he moved away from the table. He tried to include Sofie in the wave, but she was pretending to be too engrossed in something Amber was saying to notice.

Amber had just arrived though. Austin had seen her coming from the parking lot and not the church. That meant she would be going to the 10:30 mass and Sofie would be leaving alone. Austin polished off his donut and got comfortable on a bench outside the church.

****

"It doesn't look like Austin is hanging around," Amber said. She had just looked over her shoulder to see her brother leaving coffee and donuts with the donut part of the equation sticking out of his mouth.

Sofie had of course noted his departure with a mix of relief and disappointment, very common emotions when Austin was not around. She also saw the other young woman watching him leave with a hungry look on her face. Austin hadn't paid her much attention and that was both comforting and annoying. Sofie wanted to believe she'd have a better chance of getting over Austin if he'd just go ahead and find someone else. She wanted to believe it but did not. She tried to put complicated thoughts of Austin out of her head to answer Amber casually. "Perhaps you're wrong about who's avoiding whom?"

Amber shook her head. "Right now, he's only avoiding me and that's nothing new." She smiled into her cup as she inhaled the aroma. "Okay," she said as she set it down. "Saturday night you're coming over for a big croquet tournament. Invite your parents and Mr. Turner, too."

"A croquet tournament? Was this your dad's idea?"

"Would you believe it was mine?"

"Yes. But you might have to explain yourself."

"It's a compromise." Amber buried the words in a big sigh. "Every time there's any talk of planning the reception, my dad makes some hint about bringing the croquet set. I thought he was joking for a while, but then I started to worry that he was seriously planning on dragging people out to the church lawn during my wedding reception. I love my dad and I actually kind of like croquet but... no." On the last word, Amber pulled out a more serious version of her serious face than Sofie had ever seen.

"So I offered a compromise," she continued. "I told him that if he stopped mentioning croquet around my wedding then we could have a totally separate croquet event in the meantime. He got so excited about the tournament idea I am not even kidding. He already has brackets and everything. And congratulations, you're a number two seed."

Sofie stopped mid-drink so she could laugh without choking on her water. "I'm honored," she said. "I hope he's taken into account that I'm a bit out of practice."

"He's confident you and Austin are the only ones with a chance of beating him. If we start at eight, that'll give you enough time to get the shop cleaned up, right?"

"Yeah, that'll work." She lowered her voice to a whisper. "The priest is coming."

Monsignor Loy Mystery had been assigned to Sacred Heart while Sofie and Amber were in college so Sofie didn't know him well. Amber was getting to know him some during the last month because she and Joe were visiting him for premarital counseling. The man called everyone "my sheep" and Sofie thought that was just weird. But something about him – something in addition to the long, white beard – seemed to radiate a sense of knowledge. Sofie liked the idea that the guy giving the homilies was someone she could learn from so she tried to ignore the other thing.

"Greetings, my sheep," he said as he arrived at their table. "I believe this is two weeks in a row that you have visited our social time."

"That's right," Amber said, betraying her real reason with a slow, longing sip of coffee.

"Good morning, Monsignor Mystery."

He smiled at Sofie. "I know your family would give the church a good deal if we ever switched to coffee and cupcakes."

"Absolutely," she said.

"Ah." He tilted his head. "But could you help us believe cupcakes count as breakfast the way donuts do?"

"You got me there." Cupcakes would likely be less popular in the morning.

"Interesting, isn't it? Some of the things we tell ourselves." He looked thoughtful for a moment and then appeared to dismiss the thought as he turned to Amber. "Only two more Tuesdays, am I right?"

Amber nodded. "I already have my homework done. And I'm not going to tell on Joe because I think he'll be done by Tuesday." She grinned at Sofie then looked up at the priest with a playful expression.

He just kept smiling. "You two have been delightful. I must mingle some more now. Have a good day."

As he moved to a young couple by the donut table, Sofie was left wondering if he meant she and Amber were delightful or his Tuesdays with Amber and Joe.

"He prefers Monsignor Loy," Amber said.

"Oh, right. I forgot."

"He said Monsignor Mystery sounds like a cheesy detective novel."

"Great," Sofie said, "now I'm going to think that every time I see him."

"You're welcome." Amber twisted her coffee cup between her hands for a moment. "I think he must be really good at the counseling stuff because the alternative is that he's just mean."

"What makes you say that?"

"He asks hard questions, makes us think about scenarios we don't want to think about. I guess it's all about appreciating that richer and poorer or sickness and health… Those aren't just words."

"I guess it's his job to remind you you're not just planning a wedding but a life."

"I'm ready." Amber's eyes lit up and a smile seemed to bubble up from some inner glow. There was no doubt she was in love.

"Joe is a lucky guy."

"Yes, he is." Amber kept smiling, but it shifted into a more frivolous expression. "We need to put those plans on hold though while I plan a croquet party." She spent a few minutes sharing some of those plans before she finished her coffee. "I'm going to go ahead and mention it to Gran before I head to church."

Sofie nodded and grabbed both cups to dispose of on her way out. "I'll see you soon," she said.

There was a wall of heat waiting for her as Sofie stepped out of the building and out of the air conditioning. A line of trees with white flowers ran along the edge of the building between her and the sidewalk. She admired those trees until she saw the wrought iron bench in the middle of the row and Austin sitting on that bench. He was fiddling with his phone and hadn't noticed her yet.

Sofie's feet nearly came to a stop while she considered her options. She could turn around, sprint along the far edge of the parking lot and double back towards her own car. To do that, she would need to duck behind some of the parked cars in her row to avoid being seen while praying none of those cars began to back up. That was the first option.

The other option was to walk right up to Austin and give him what he seemed to want, which was to prove they could have a casual, non-awkward conversation. Sofie's legs felt as uncoordinated as a toddler as she convinced herself to take the more mature option. It was probably impossible to embarrass herself any more than she already had. And there was a good chance he hadn't thought about it every day for the past year like she had. Perhaps *he* could have a conversation that was not awkward.

6 PAST

I t was picture day. Not the day that pictures were taken but the day they came home. Sofie was nervous. Her 7th grade picture captured her cross-eyed. She had them retaken and the first batch fed the shredder before anyone else saw them. There had been no real harm, but she was still hoping for a better experience this year.

Her last period teacher was handing them out and he'd waited so long the bell rang before they were all distributed. Half the class left while the other half gathered around him to better hear their names in the chaos. Sofie grabbed her envelope and slammed it face down on top of her books without looking at the picture. She rushed into the hallway and peeked at it by her locker.

It was okay. She was probably not the most photogenic girl in her class, but there were no obvious flaws. Relieved, she finished packing up and went to find Amber. Sofie worked at her parents' bakery after school a few days each week and went home with Amber most other days.

"How's your picture?" Amber asked as they met to board the bus. She knew Sofie had been worried.

"Better than last year's."

"Good. Can I see it?"

"Yeah." Sofie took a seat on the bus and slid over to make room for Amber as she unzipped her backpack. Amber showed her picture as well before they both put them away again.

When they got to Amber's house, she unlocked the door, hung her backpack on a hook just inside the door, and then yelled, "Mom?"

Amber's mom had gotten a new job a few months earlier and now worked from home about half the time. Amber couldn't follow her schedule and always wanted to know first thing whether or not she was in the house. It wasn't as though Amber was in a hurry to break all the rules if her mom wasn't there. She just liked to know.

Sofie understood. She'd like to be able to yell Austin's name as soon as she came in but had to wait for him to show himself or not. She'd miss him most of the winter because he played basketball. It was still fall so the odds were good he was there somewhere.

Amber's mom's voice floated from an office around the corner. "I'm home. How was school, girls?"

"Fine," Amber said. "We got pictures today."

"Put yours on the counter with Austin's. I've been waiting for them to give both pictures to the grandparents."

"Okay." Amber turned to Sofie. "Can you do that for me? I need a bathroom."

"Sure." Sofie opened her friend's backpack while Amber dashed upstairs. She knew right where the pictures were, and she was almost as familiar with Amber's house as she was with her own. She slipped into the quiet kitchen and put the envelope next to a stack of pictures of Austin. They'd already been cut apart. The high school pictures must have come home earlier in the week.

Sofie picked up a wallet size picture to get a better look. Temptation coursed through her. She shouldn't though. Someone might figure out it was her. She put the picture back down but couldn't take her eyes off it. Austin looked good in green. Who was she kidding? She thought he looked good in every color.

She was still standing in that corner of the kitchen when Amber returned. "Sounds like Dillon is here, too," she said. "I bet they come down when they realize we're home. I think he likes you." She whispered the last line.

Sofie shook her head with doubt. She hadn't noticed anything to suggest that. Then again, her attention was usually elsewhere so the signs might have been easy to miss.

"I think he does," Amber said. Heavy footsteps could be heard on the stairs. She grinned as though that proved her point.

"Hey." Dillon walked into the kitchen ahead of Austin. "We were thinking of playing *Uno*. It's more fun with four."

Amber opened her mouth for what was surely agreement but then realized Austin had already begun to deal out four hands. "We haven't agreed to anything yet," she said.

Austin rolled his eyes at her protest. "You'll play if Sofie plays, and we all know I can talk Sofie into playing."

"Maybe not." Sofie crossed her arms. Of course Austin could talk her into spending time with him, but he didn't have to be so smug about it.

When the cards were dealt, Dillon took the seat next to Austin. Both guys looked up expectantly at the girls. Amber copied Sofie's defiant posture. "You could at least ask nicely," she said.

Dillon looked at Austin to take the lead on how to persuade them. Austin got up from the table and walked over to Sofie. He leaned close enough to whisper in her ear. "Eenie-meenie-miney-moser."

As his warm breath tickled her neck, Sofie shivered and melted at the same time. He was so close she couldn't stand it. She nearly ran to the table, glad once again for a stupid nickname. It was better than Austin knowing the real reason she was putty in his hands. She was sure she was blushing and that wasn't because of the nickname either.

Dillon thought it was. He shook his head with something like disbelief mixed with envy. "Man, I wish you'd tell me what you have on her."

"I can't tell you," Austin said, "because then I'd lose my power." He followed Sofie back to the table and all three of them looked at Amber.

She still had her arms folded across her chest but clearly wanted to play.

Austin sighed. "Amber, would you please give us the pleasure of your company for a rousing game of cards?"

She couldn't hold back the laugh despite his mocking tone. She came over to pick up her cards. Sofie tried to pay more attention to Dillon than usual. He did seem to be looking at her a lot during the game. It may have been because she was looking at him. And it may have been because there was some truth in Amber's suspicion. Sofie was a little flattered just in case.

But she knew it wouldn't amount to anything. He'd get over her soon enough. That was how crushes were supposed to work. Amber had confided interest in at least half a dozen guys over the last two years. Sofie was the only one who couldn't shake a crush. Sofie was the only one who always had the same person on her mind, a person who would forever be off limits.

She and Dillon were both invited to stay for dinner that night. Afterwards, Amber's mom asked if Sofie was ready to go home.

"Yeah. Thanks for driving me."

"Anytime," Mrs. Waits said. "We love having you and we understand running a business keeps people busy."

Sofie nodded and looked at Amber. She was the only one who knew why Sofie's mom couldn't pick her up. Sofie had thought she didn't want anyone at all to know, but the sympathy behind Amber's encouraging smile made her relieved there was one person who did know. She waved to her friend, took a last glance at Austin and collected her school things. The drive was only five minutes and she thanked Mrs. Waits again as she got out of her car.

Sofie hung up her backpack and went cautiously into her parents' bedroom. Her mom was sitting on the floor with her back against the side of the bed. She had a wet towel on her head and a bucket cradled in one arm. She was holding a magazine she wasn't reading in the other hand.

"Not a good day, huh?" Sofie whispered.

Her mom shook her head – slowly – before she forced a smile. "Don't look so worried, honey. If the medicine is treating the cancer half as bad as the rest of me, I'll have no trouble beating it."

Sofie nodded at the already familiar mantra. "Do you need anything?"

"I'm okay."

Sofie nodded again and quietly left the room. The one thing she knew she could do for her mom was to leave her alone. That way she didn't try to pretend she was any less miserable than she really was.

Sofie's bedroom was right across the hall. She went inside and turned on some music. If her mom needed to vomit again, she didn't want to hear it. Sofie sank down to the floor and leaned against the side of her own bed. She felt horrible and not only because of her mom. She'd never stolen anything before and now she was a thief. She knew they had extras, and she knew that didn't make it okay.

Carefully, she leaned forward to pull the picture out of her back pocket. Austin had looked directly into the camera and it seemed as though he was looking at her now. Looking at her and smiling. Sofie felt sure it was her heart, the actual muscle responsible for keeping her alive, that twinged as she stared into his eyes. She wished she could be somewhere else with him right now. Anywhere else. The music wasn't loud enough.

7 PRESENT

"Sofie Ennemoser, you can do this." Sofie whispered the words, giving herself a pep talk as she approached Austin.

He took one hand off his phone and scratched the side of his head. A chunk of hair was left sticking out beside his ear. Sofie smiled to herself. Austin's hair was only slightly wavy and if he let it get too long, it would start behaving erratically. She thought most guys would either get more frequent haircuts or turn to some sort of styling product to solve the problem. Austin didn't seem to notice there was a problem.

His phone rang in his hand and Sofie picked up her pace as he answered it. Maybe she could get away with a wave if he was busy. He looked up at her with recognition and resolve. She heard him say, "Hi, Dad. I'm going to call you back in a few minutes. Okay?" He stood in front of her and stuffed the phone into his pocket. "Hi, Sofie."

"Hi, Austin. You were up early this morning."

"I guess so. You... uh... you wanna sit for a minute?" He gestured back to the bench he'd just vacated. "It's nice out here."

"I guess so." Sofie pulled in a breath and tucked her skirt under her legs as she sat. Surely this wouldn't be as uncomfortable as she feared. Austin had tried to help. He'd called her a few times during her last semester to say hello and to prepare them both for facing each other. That's what he had said the first time he called. Sort of. He'd said, "I know you're coming back to Thompsonville soon and Amber won't let us get away with not talking. I thought we should get an early start."

Sofie had handled those phone calls fairly well. Austin was great. He was easy to talk to when he was only words floating through a phone. Now, however, he was not just words. He was the eyes that still watched her from a stolen picture. He was the first mouth she'd ever kissed. And he was at least a dozen mannerisms so familiar she couldn't forget them no matter how hard she tried.

"How are the cake pops doing?" Austin asked.

"Not bad. I... I sometimes feel guilty that most of the ones we sell are to kids who come in with their parents and beg for one."

"Did the shop change much since last summer?"

"No." Sofie hesitated. "I mean a little but I visited a few times so I kept up." She'd managed to avoid Austin on those visits.

"Have you worked out a regular schedule with your parents now? I imagine they get a little more time off with you around."

"We're kind of in the busy season still but soon I think. Your work is... uh... fine?"

"Fine. Yes. No one's done anything too stupid lately."

"Glad to hear that," Sofie said. Austin worked in human resources and liked to tell stories that proved humans were not always a good resource.

"Is Amber getting on your nerves yet with all the wedding talk?"

Sofie could hear in his voice that it was getting on *his* nerves. "No. It is – hopefully – a once-in-a-lifetime event. I'm excited to see how it all comes together."

"Really not at all?" He dipped his chin and looked up at her with doubting eyes that were so attractive she had to look away and let him think he caught some dishonesty.

"Really not at all," she insisted anyway. "I'm happy for Amber."

"I know a wedding is a big deal. But you can't tell me you weren't starting to daydream even a little the other day when she spent fifteen minutes describing the pattern on a piece of lace."

Sofie laughed and then stopped herself. "You're exaggerating."

"Am I?"

She took a quick peek at his amused expression and wanted a less affecting topic. He'd mentioned a move the last time they talked before her graduation. "How's the new place?" she asked.

"Uh..." He seemed to be searching for something to say. "It's a lot closer to my parents so I'm cooking less often. But it's a bit farther from work." He pointed to the large brick building. "Closer to church."

"So you judge the place solely on distances?"

He shrugged. "It's quieter. I guess that's good." He'd moved from a fairly large complex to a simple duplex.

"Have you met your neighbor?" Sofie asked.

"No. I think I have one though."

"You *think* you have a neighbor?"

"There's a truck, a gray truck, that's regularly parked on that side and I'm assuming it belongs to a neighbor, but I've never actually seen anyone."

"And you've been there like six or eight weeks now?"

"About that," Austin said. "I guess he or she is a keep-to-yourself kind of person."

"That's what they say about serial killers."

Austin smiled slightly. "People could probably say that about me."

"So maybe you don't have anything to worry about."

"I don't think so. Living next to someone exactly like me would obviously be a pleasure."

Of course he was kidding, but Sofie agreed with the thought so strongly – internally – that she had to escape his presence. She'd done enough to show she wasn't avoiding him. She stood from the bench. "I should probably get going."

"Sofie?" Austin jumped from the bench and took a step to place himself in her path. "You're working on Saturday, right?"

"Yeah."

"But not so late you can't do something fun afterwards?"

"Of course not. Amber already told me about the croquet tournament."

"Right. The croquet tournament." Austin formed the words slowly, as though he couldn't quite believe they were participating in such a thing. Sofie didn't blame him, but she still expected it to be fun.

"I haven't played in months though," she said, "so no gloating if you beat me."

"If?" Austin put on a cheeky grin. "You haven't played in ages and you still think there's a chance you're going to beat me?"

When they'd played in the past, Austin undeniably won more often, but Sofie kept it competitive and won games now and then. It wasn't completely out of the question that she could beat him now. "I haven't seen the brackets," she said. "It's possible your dad will take us both out anyway." She sidestepped into the parking lot as she talked, away from Austin. "I'll see you Saturday then."

"Sofie, wait a minute."

She waved without looking back. "I really gotta go." She walked quickly to her car and turned back only once she was safely inside it. Austin waved but even from a distance she could see the frustration on his face. It made her feel guilty. He was trying so hard for things to go back to normal between them, and she just couldn't do it. She couldn't pretend he didn't know how she felt.

8 PAST

S ofie was not a fan of poetry. Most of the time, she didn't get it. The poetry she was studying in her 9th grade English class fell into the category of most of the time. Her teacher, Mr. Feckley, dismissed meter, rhyme, alliteration and all the other techniques that Sofie had so far associated with what made a poem a poem. The lines he introduced to the class seemed to consist of words on paper that said one thing and meant something else.

She was staring numbly at the latest work. Mr. Feckley was giving the class time to "digest" the poem. Sofie had read it three times in search of something intelligent to contribute to a discussion.

So far the only thing she'd come up with was to point out that the title – Winter – was a word that did not appear anywhere else in the poem. Mr. Feckley had warned them several times during this poetry unit not to overlook titles and he got excited over sparse wording. There might be something significant about the title. If he asked any follow-up questions though, Sofie would not have a clue *what* was significant.

"Pay special attention to lines three and four," he was telling the class now. "Those are arguably the most powerful lines."

Sofie concentrated on those lines.

> A hole so deep the bottom taunts me
> with its nothingness. Its comfort is without.

Nothingness? It was a poem about nothing? But Mr. Feckley liked poems that meant something other than what they said so maybe it was about… something? Something that was nothing or wasn't nothing? Sofie shook the unhelpful thoughts out of her head and waited for the explanation.

Mr. Feckley sighed at the blank looks he was getting. "This is a poem about loss," he said. "The loss of someone dear to you, more specifically. The author wrote this piece about a month after his mother passed away."

Sofie read the poem again while a boy in the middle of the room raised his hand. "Shouldn't a poem make sense without having to read the author's biography?"

That was a fair point in Sofie's opinion but biography or not, she suddenly understood the poem. Her mother's doctor was optimistic, but she was about to have some important tests and Sofie understood that these words were her greatest fear. She flew from her seat and grabbed a whiteboard eraser with Mr. Feckley's name on it as she ran from the room. It was a bathroom pass. She was supposed to ask before she used it, but she'd rather he believed she had a bathroom emergency than know she was crying.

The nearest bathroom was right around the corner. As she rounded that corner though, she saw a dozen or so students milling about the hallway outside it. She didn't want to go through them. She turned around and sat on the floor before the corner with her back to the wall and her knees as close to her face as she could get them. The tears fell hard, and she felt like a moron. She hadn't cried the whole time her mom had been sick and now a stupid poem got to her.

A pair of feet appeared out of the corner of her eye and the tears slowed against the shock of recognition. She knew those shoes. Austin had those shoes. It couldn't be Austin though. It had to be someone else, anyone else. Austin was the last person she wanted to see her as a sniffling, snot-faced mess.

The person quietly sat down next to her and she knew it was Austin without looking at him. He was perfectly familiar. She pulled her arms over her head to hide.

"Do you want me to get someone?" he whispered.

She shook her head.

"Do you want me to go away?"

She did. She did *not* want him to see her like this. She felt her head shaking anyway. "Why aren't you in class?"

"I... uh... I'm sorry. I couldn't hear you."

Sofie loosened her arms to unbury her face without revealing it. "Why aren't you in class?" she repeated.

"I have chemistry now. He told us to wait in the hall while he set up some sort of experiment. I think he didn't want us to see the bottles he was taking things from."

She hoped he'd be called back to class before a teacher came out and demanded to know why she was sitting in the hallway. But she really liked having him sit next to her as long as he couldn't see her face. She'd stopped crying but didn't have a tissue and knew she'd be red and puffy.

Austin said nothing for what felt like a long time. She heard him swallow before he very quietly asked, "Is this about... your mom?"

Sofie gasped. "Amber promised—"

"She didn't tell me. I'm sure she hasn't told anyone."

"Then how did you know?"

"Your mom called our mom a while back. She knew you asked Amber not to tell anyone and she wanted our mom to know the secret she was keeping in case... She thought it might be hard on her. Then Mom told me because..." He sighed. "It's insulting really. She told me because she wanted me to be nice to you. I'm always nice, right?" He bumped her arm with his.

Sofie knew he was joking because he teased her and generally treated her no better than he treated his sister. But she thought that was wonderful and found herself smiling inside her little arm-cave.

Austin couldn't see the smile so he bumped her arm again. "Have I ever not been nice to you, Eenie-meenie-miney-moser?"

Her body shook with something other than a sob and she knew Austin could tell it was a giggle. A door opened around the corner and his teacher called his class back into the room.

"Gotta go," Austin said as he stood. He said something else as he walked away and at first she thought it was, "I'll leave you alone." But that didn't seem right and after a minute, she realized he had said, "You'll never be alone."

And with his words came a much better understanding of that poem. The person who wrote it had no faith. He'd written of a grief with nothingness, with no hope of being together again. There was grief with God and there was pain, but there was never nothing. Sofie's dad had tried to explain that to her several times, and she hadn't gotten it before.

For some reason, the insight made Sofie laugh. She pictured trying to explain to Mr. Feckley that sometimes the hallway could be more educational than a classroom. He would probably not accept that excuse for running out of his class.

Sofie ducked into the bathroom as soon as the hallway was clear of Austin's classmates. She washed her face and stared at her reflection, trying to give the red around her eyes a minute to fade. She tried to slip back into class unnoticed. It almost worked because her seat was near the door. The girl next to her asked what happened and Sofie said only, "Bathroom," which was not a lie as she had indeed visited the bathroom.

Mr. Feckley said nothing right then. A new poem had appeared on her desk, and the class was silently studying it. This one read as though it was an ode to sand. It was, in fact, called An Ode to Sand. Mr. Feckley tried to explain how it was actually about time. Sofie didn't get it. She wasn't the only one. Most of her classmates walked out still scratching their heads when the bell rang.

Mr. Feckley called Sofie's name as she tried to leave. She worried he was going to reprimand her for not getting permission to leave class. He only asked if she was feeling better.

Neither Sofie nor Austin ever told the rest of his family – or anyone else as far as she knew – what happened in the hallway. They all continued to pretend Amber was the only one who knew what was happening with Sofie's mom. Until Sofie finally had good news. When she came into Amber's house bursting with the announcement that it was officially remission, she was so relieved the family could share her joy without a need to be filled in on the backstory.

Amber spun her around in a circle, jumping up and down so much she almost clocked Sofie's nose with her forehead. Both girls were laughing too much to care. When Amber finally let go, her mom was waiting with her arms out to embrace Sofie, too. Mrs. Waits' tears were contagious because Sofie felt her eyes leaking despite the smile still plastered to her face.

Mr. Waits claimed the next hug. He squeezed so tightly Sofie wasn't sure she had any emotion left. Everything that didn't come out through the laughter or tears was forced out through the comforting pressure. The peace she'd begun to feel in her life seemed fuller.

But then she realized that everyone was looking uncertainly at Austin. He was the only one who hadn't hugged her, and his family seemed to be deciding if he needed to jump on that bandwagon. His mom tipped her head and her eyes, encouraging Austin towards Sofie. Sofie's face flamed as she told herself this might be her one chance to throw herself into his arms and not have anyone suspect romantic feelings prompted it. She wanted to go for it. But Austin wasn't much of a hugger. Would he mind?

Mr. Waits said, "Suck it up and hug her, son. It's a happy occasion."

"All right." Austin smiled wryly at Sofie. "I dare you to hug me, too."

He took a step backwards to keep his balance as she hit his chest. His hands softly patted her back. Sofie studied the fabric of Austin's shirt and inhaled deeply through her nose to fix the moment with more of her senses. She wanted to save it as a memory she could look back on and draw strength from for years. For once his hold on her was physical, and her soul flew from its usual constraints for one splendid moment.

Later, as it dawned on Amber that her family seemed to know what she hadn't told them, Sofie explained that their moms had been talking without mentioning how she knew that. She liked too much that she had a secret with Austin.

9 PRESENT

T he aroma of warm chocolate frosting overpowered Sofie's senses. She dipped another ball of cake into the mixture then held it over the pan, twisting the stick until it stopped dripping. She pushed the stick handle into a hole to hold it upright before she picked up another one. She used to like making cake pops. They smelled so good and she could handle the simple swirl decorations without asking for help.

The process was less enjoyable today because it was the first time she made a batch since Austin had asked about them. He'd said, "How are the cake pops doing?" That was all. His passing interest was all it took to fill her head with things she didn't want to think.

First on the list was how wonderful it would be to invite him to the bakery to help her make them. She thought of showing him how to ball up the crumbs around the stick. She dipped one into the chocolate coating and imagined how near Austin would have to stand to dip one at the same time. She could almost feel his arm coming around her waist the way her dad did when he stood in close quarters with her mom.

Her distraction caused Sofie to dunk one farther into the pan. Nearly an inch of chocolate wrapped the stick below the cake and it stuck out as a mistake when she pressed it into the holder by the others. Austin would tease her about that if he was there. He'd probably ask to eat one while it was still warm and suggest her imperfect pop was begging to be eaten early. She could picture herself telling him he had to wait, that he couldn't eat one until she decorated them. He'd probably say that was nonsense, that the little white swirls didn't change the taste much. Then he'd dare her to try to convince him she'd never tasted a warm one herself.

Sofie knew for a fact that they were delicious before the coating had time to set. She'd relent and offer Austin an unfinished cake pop. But maybe he wouldn't just take it from her. Maybe he'd put his hand over hers and bring it to his mouth to kiss her fingers before he tasted the dessert.

"Where are you today, my dear?"

Sofie startled and took in the reality of the moment. She was absently twirling an empty stick between her fingers and Mr. Turner, who had just made her jump, was standing by her elbow with an expression that said he may have been watching her for some time.

Her face was already flushed and she silently rebuked Austin. Why did he have to bring up the cake pops? Why did he have to give her yet another excuse to think about him? She was trying to limit her thoughts to friendship. That fantasy was... not. It was decidedly outside the limits of friendship. She resolved not to let Austin into her head at all for the rest of the day.

"Daydreaming I guess," she said to Mr. Turner. "You won't tell the boss, right?"

"Mum's the word." He pressed his finger lightly to his lips to emphasize the point. "Three cakes left to be picked up and twenty minutes to close," he said. "What do you suppose are the odds we'll have someone banging on the door while we're cleaning up?"

"I hope low," she said. "I don't know why, but it creeps me out to let people in after we've closed." It was a weird thing to admit. They had strangers coming in and out all day and she never felt uneasy. Somehow it was different once the door had been locked.

"It's the lights," Mr. Turner said.

"The lights?"

"We turn out the front lights when we lock the door. The dimmer lighting makes this place feel more intimate, makes letting people in feel sort of... invasive."

"Wow." Sofie blinked as the understanding sank in. "I think you're right."

He smiled thoughtfully. "It's almost romantic. If someone who looked like my Jannie came in, I might not mind it."

Janet – or Jannie – was the late Mrs. Turner. They had been married less than three years when she and their son died in childbirth. Sofie cringed yet again to remember how her initial reaction to his history had been incredulous rather than sympathetic. She'd thought no one had died that way in at least a hundred years. Being only thirteen years old at the time now felt like a poor excuse for her ignorance. She also marveled that, despite the tragedy, he always smiled when he talked about his wife.

"Have you, um… have you ever thought about getting married again?"

"I have thought about it from time to time." He picked up a tube of white frosting to add those swirls to the first cake pops as he talked. "It was years before I was willing to entertain the possibility. And then I didn't want to get married only because I wanted a child. I simply never found another woman who… fit."

"I'm sorry that you never… I mean, that your son…"

Mr. Turner nodded as though he appreciated the sentiment she was tripping over. "At least I have had the pleasure of watching you grow up, my dear. I still remember how angry you were when your parents hired me."

"You could tell?" Sofie bit her lower lip in a remorseful expression. She thought she'd hid her resentment better.

He smiled. "You thought you'd be running this place by yourself before you were out of middle school. You were certain my help was unnecessary."

"I suppose I was a bit…" Sofie just stopped and laughed at herself, rather than choose a word to describe her adolescent folly. She peeled off her plastic gloves after placing the last stick in the holder and began to clean up.

"Turns out God had good timing," Mr. Turner said. "I didn't know how much I needed to be needed, and you didn't know about your mom."

"I did come to see your usefulness."

"Grudgingly." He winked at her. "But now I think you might even miss me."

"Of course I… Oh! I forgot to ask how the trial run went."

He appeared to consider his answer before he said, "Some minor bumps, but I made it through the night and so did the camper." Mr. Turner had recently bought an RV as part of his retirement plan and visited a local campsite to practice.

"Where do you think you'll go first?" Sofie asked.

"Perhaps I will throw darts at a map."

She shook her head disapprovingly. "That's not how you plan a trip."

"What if I let you throw them?"

"I'd aim for Thompsonville," she said with a smile.

He laughed. "You got to go away for school. It's only fair I get my turn. But I won't leave before Labor Day. I believe fall might be better for camping anyway."

She conceded his point, both of them actually, and took the frosting to finish the swirls while he stepped away to help a customer. That was one of the three cakes out the door. The second was picked up immediately after the first. Mr. Turner pulled the last one out of the cooler and held it while he faced the door expectantly.

"Five more minutes," Sofie said. "Are they going to make it?"

"I think so. I'm thinking positive thoughts about," he looked down to read the cake, "Alexander's birthday."

"Maybe it's tomorrow. Maybe this will be one of those frantic morning pick-ups."

"No." Mr. Turner looked at the door. "Someone will be here any second for this cake."

Sofie looked through the glass on the front door. No one was reaching for that handle. No one was in sight at all. Then she looked at the clock. Four minutes before the door was locked.

Mr. Turner smiled at her. "Don't think about locking up early just to prove me wrong."

"Never." Sofie pretended to be shocked at the accusation. "I want Alexander to have a happy birthday, too."

He lifted the cake slightly in his hands as though getting ready to hand it over to an invisible customer.

Sofie laughed. "Hello, Alexander's mom. We're so glad you got here in time to get his cake. How old is Alexander this year?" She paused and then nodded. "That's such a good age. I hope he'll enjoy the cake. Oh, you love it? Thank you." Another pause for their imaginary customer. "Yes. Race cars are Mr. Turner's specialty." She glanced at the man with the cake and he was trying not to laugh.

"Are you finished?" he asked.

"I guess so. We still have a cake though."

"I happen to know a sure-fire way to get this picked up."

"Put it back in the cooler?"

"Of course." He left to put the cake away and Sofie followed with her tray of cake pops.

The bell chimed to signal a customer exactly ten seconds after the cake was stored for the night. Mr. Turner greeted the man, who was in fact Alexander's dad, and handled the last transaction. Then he shut off the lights to begin closing the shop for the night.

Sofie slipped into the office to answer the phone. It was only someone wanting to know their hours. She should have quickly returned to wash that frosting pan. Her mom had left a sketch of a croquet-themed cake on the desk. It made her think of Austin. No matter what, croquet would always make her think of Austin. She hated the game the first few times she tried it and kept playing only because it was an excuse to be with him. Now she liked the game. She'd never be as nutty about it as Austin's dad – probably no one would – but she liked it enough to have her own, as yet unused, set of mallets in her apartment.

If only she could invite Austin over to break it in. Their brief time alone outside the church proved she wasn't ready for that. She also failed in her resolution to not think about him again. It had taken twenty minutes to break through that resolve. She pushed thoughts of Austin and her failure to not think about Austin from her head and focused on the cake sketch. Her mom was so talented. Then her personal phone rang.

Austin. Of course it was Austin. He was calling for the first time since Sofie had been back from school and trying to pretend she wasn't avoiding him. She would not avoid his call. "Hi, Austin."

"Sofie. All closed up for the day?"

"Yeah."

"You heading home then?"

"I should be. I got distracted by a croquet cake."

His laugh was deep. It rumbled through the phone and into her fingers. "What's a bouquet cake?" he asked.

"Croquet. My mom's making one for Saturday."

"Oh. Sadly, that makes sense to me. Why is it distracting you?"

"She left a sketch of her plan for it and..." Sofie hesitated. Was he looking for the long answer or the short answer? He called. He was the one who thought they should talk. "It's good. I'm looking at this picture and wondering if I could ever... I think I could make this. I'm getting the hang of most of the decorating even if it does take me three times as long as anyone else here and maybe several scraped off mistakes, but I can make a cake look nice. Eventually. From a picture. But what if I never figure out how to make the picture to begin with? What if twenty years from now my mom wants to retire and someone comes in here asking for some sort of crazy never before done cake and I don't know where to start?"

"Wow, Sofie. Those are like... late Sunday night thoughts not early Thursday evening thoughts."

"What?" His answer made no sense but laughing at it made her feel better so it was a great answer.

"I mean there are times when deep contemplation leads to, you know, epiphanies or insights. And there are times when it upsets you for no reason. Do you want me to tell you all the reasons you shouldn't worry?"

Her voice had barely quivered, and he still heard her developing anxiety. She knew she would remember this moment the next time she vowed not to think about Austin. Darn it. He could be *so* annoying. "Go ahead," she said.

"Number one, you can and will learn a lot in twenty years. Number two, you can store pictures of all your mom's cakes between now and then. Number three, if you're still making cakes in twenty years, I highly doubt anyone could request something you haven't seen. Case in point... You're looking at a croquet cake. Number... where was I?"

"Four. But I get it."

"Doesn't matter," he said. "I'm not done. Number four, you can always ask the customer to draw a picture of what he or she wants. Number five, God will help you. Number six, so will all your friends. We all know you're better than you think—"

"I get it." She needed him to stop. He just included himself as her friend. That was sweet and scary, both what she wanted and didn't. "I'll save serious thoughts for Sundays from now on."

"Good," he said, satisfaction around the word. "So are you making the cake for Saturday?"

"No. I'll have my mom handle it since it's such an important event for your dad. And for Amber, to keep him focused on a proper reception."

"Yeah." Austin spoke slowly, trying to voice a thought carefully. "Do you... do you ever think maybe you worry too much about keeping Amber happy?"

"Of course not. She's my best friend and I have to counteract all the stuff you do to bother her."

"You're smiling, aren't you? You like it when I bother Amber."

Yes. She was smiling. "No, I'm not. I like it when people are nice to each other."

"There will be a lot of nice people at my parents' house on Saturday, right?"

"Yeah."

"And we'll both be there, being nice."

"Okay."

"And... would you get mad if I tried to call it a date?"

She nearly hung up on him.

She didn't. She gathered some self-control. "No. But that's not funny yet. I really should help Mr. Turner clean up. I'll see you Saturday. Bye." He was saying something when she disconnected the call so perhaps she hung up on him after all. But only after she said bye and he almost deserved it. Austin may have recovered enough to make light of what happened, but Sofie could not.

"I do hope, my dear, that whatever troubles you will be resolved before I leave."

Sofie startled for the second time that day at Mr. Turner's voice and then sighed at his worried expression. "Not you, too," she said.

"Does that mean you've noticed your parents' concern?"

A somewhat derisive laugh escaped her throat. "It would be hard not to. Mom keeps asking if I want to talk and Dad keeps looking at me like he's terrified I might want to talk."

"I take it then that there's nothing any of us can do to help."

"Not unless you can reverse time or maybe put some words back in my mouth."

"How popular would I be if I had that talent?"

He'd gone from worried to amused in less than a second, and it caused Sofie to brighten as well. "I believe people would be lined up for your help."

"Your problem is, at least in some way, a common one."

"Not in any way that makes me feel better." Humiliation, apparently, didn't love company.

10 PAST

Something was up with Amber. She came home from school alone, which was already weird for a Tuesday. Austin was sitting at one end of the couch trying to finish a book for school. It was dull and had a lot of confusing Russian names. He would not have minded having an excuse to put the book down, but Amber was alone.

Rather than make a point of being in a different room, she walked over and slumped on the opposite end of the couch. She mostly stared at the wall and appeared deep in thought but occasionally cast a glance at Austin as though he was doing something to annoy her. He had a really bad feeling that he had become her last resort.

Someone had asked Amber to the prom. All she'd been able to talk about since was how excited she was and how completely unfair their parents were by saying she could only go if she went with at least one other couple. Of course she wanted Sofie to go. They were sophomores though and only juniors and seniors could buy tickets so she needed an older date. Amber was sure that wouldn't be a problem. She didn't seem to notice that Sofie was not as enthusiastic as she was.

Amber emptied her lungs in a huff and then narrowed her eyes at Austin. He closed the book, figuring he might as well get this conversation over with. "Where's Sofie today?" he asked.

"We had a fight."

That was surprising. As far as he knew, a fight was a first for Sofie and Amber. Perhaps her mood had nothing to do with the prom. He opened the book again. Amber kept talking.

"She told me today that she's already been asked to the prom… twice. She turned them both down!"

Austin kept his book open to look unconcerned. But he was relieved. Relieved and too curious for his own good. "Did she say why?"

"She said…" Amber paused to glare at a spot in the carpet. "She said she wasn't that interested in the prom and she turned them down before she knew I needed her to go and now she'd feel bad if she agreed to go with someone else after she turned down the other guys so she's going to say no even if someone else asks her."

Amber put her face in her hands and her long hair fell forward like a curtain. Her voice came out mumbled, but Austin could still understand her. "It will be so humiliating if I have to tell James I can't go with him now," she said. "I wanted to make it sound like I just wanted to go with a group and not that I *had* to. Now I can't really think of anyone we could go with except…"

Austin turned the page he hadn't read as though he didn't pick up on her implication. He knew the question was going to come anyway.

After a minute of silence, Amber said only, "Please, Austin."

He sighed and put down the book. "No," he said. "Absolutely not. There is no way I am going to the prom as my sister's chaperone."

"Not a chaperone." She turned to him hopefully. "Just a double date."

"I really don't think that's any better."

"Come on, Austin. Please. I know it could be a challenge to find a girl willing to go with you but—"

"I don't think you want to insult me while asking a favor."

"Sorry," she said. "Habit. Have you asked anyone?"

"Not that it's any of your business, but no. I'm not interested in going to the prom at all. With or without you."

"What if I made it worth your while?"

She was willing to bribe him? "Do you even like this James guy?" he asked.

She gave a very unconvincing shrug. "I barely know him."

"Then why do you want to go so bad?"

"Because it's the prom."

"You can go next year."

Amber put her head down again. "You wouldn't understand."

"You're right about that." He returned to his boring book because he thought the conversation was over. He had, after all, said no.

"I'm not like Sofie," Amber said softly. "I'm too… quiet to get noticed at school. I don't think anyone will ever ask me again."

Austin said nothing. He still didn't see the big deal about the prom. He only had one friend who was going and only because he had a girlfriend who wanted to go.

"I have a plan," Amber said.

A plan that apparently involved her brother. That was the only reason she'd share it with him. Austin said, "No," without looking up from his book.

"I haven't told you yet."

"No," he said again.

Amber plowed ahead. "You and Sofie can go together. With me."

This plan had the effect of getting Austin's full attention, and all he could do was pretend that was because he thought it was ridiculous and not because he was tempted by it. "You can't get either one of us to go so your plan is to get both of us to go?"

"Just listen," Amber said. "Sofie doesn't want to go only because she doesn't like that she has to have a date." She pointed at him. "*You're* not a date so that solves her problem. I'm prepared to do whatever it takes to talk you into going, but I'd feel bad if some girl found out that you only asked her because I bribed you. Sofie won't care. She knows how bad I want to go. So the only thing that remains is for you and me to negotiate a price."

Austin simply stared at his sister. She was serious. That much he knew. But *she* didn't know how bad her plan was. It was a terrible, terrible plan because he was already thinking about Sofie way more than he should. Signing up to spend more time with her was only going to get him in trouble. He couldn't stop the curiosity though. "Have you shared this plan with Sofie?"

"That's why she's not here."

"I thought that was because you two had a fight."

"No." Amber rolled her eyes as though it wasn't her fault he thought that. "We made up. But she thought you might get mad when I asked you, and she only wanted to deal with one fight today."

"So she... agreed?"

"Sort of. She said she'd go if you would, but I think she doubted my persuasiveness."

Austin laughed. "I'm doubting your persuasiveness at the moment, too."

"All right," Amber said, "let's do this." She set her jaw and gave him a fierce look. "Prom is almost three weeks away. I will do all your chores between now and then *and* I will pay for you and Sofie's tickets."

It was not a good idea to give in to his sister. It was not a good idea for their parents to find out he was taking advantage of her desperation. They would certainly find out. And it was not a good idea to think about Sofie at all. But the dominating thought in Austin's head was that Sofie would look very nice dressed up for prom. "Paying for the tickets is a given," he said.

"I will also wash your car." Amber was not backing down.

"We're only talking about the dance here, right? No dinner or flowers or any... I don't know what else."

"Just the dance," Amber said. She could tell he was caving and was trying to hold back a smile. "And you don't even have to dance. You just have to be there."

"You better do a good job on my car," Austin said.

Amber stopped holding back and jumped off the couch and up and down several times. "I'm going to call Sofie right now." She ran upstairs and left Austin regretting most of their conversation.

Doug and Charlene Waits were not thrilled with the arrangement, but they let Amber and Austin's deal stand. Austin only felt guilty about it when he saw Sofie helping Amber wash his car. A little guilty and a little annoyed that Amber was getting off easy. They were having an awful lot of fun throwing sponges around the yard.

Sofie came over early the day of the prom to get ready with Amber. They must have had something else going on as well because it took hours. Austin met some guys for a game of basketball at the park. He came home and had dinner and a shower and the girls were still hiding out in Amber's room.

Amber eventually came down grinning and Sofie was right behind her. Her hair was curly, which was different. Austin was not normally a fan of different. Sofie was pretty enough to pull off different. Her dress was long and bright green and had short lacey sleeves. Mostly he liked it because it fit her very well. Amber's dress was pink, and that was about the only thing he noticed about it.

His mom made a sound like the air being squeezed out of a balloon as the girls hit the bottom of the stairs. "You both look so beautiful," she said. "Over here for pictures." She snapped picture after picture for a minute before she waved Austin over like an afterthought.

Amber sighed. "Mom, he's not even dressed."

"I'm ready," Austin said to give his sister a hard time. He was dressed except for his jacket and tie, which everyone could see draped over a chair.

Amber was not in the mood. She started tapping her foot at him. "Put it on," she said.

He put the tie around his neck.

Amber made an impatient grunt.

"I'm working on it," he said, adding a little impatience of his own.

"You can't wear that tie," she said. "It looks like you're going to a funeral."

"It's the only tie I own. Buying a new tie was not part of the deal."

"Put it down." Amber started back up the stairs. "I'll get one of Dad's."

Austin looked around the room for other opinions on what was admittedly a boring gray and navy striped tie. He kind of thought ties were supposed to be boring.

His dad shrugged at him.

His mom very diplomatically said, "It is a bit sedate."

Austin held the tie up to Sofie.

She didn't look at it. She winced apologetically and said, "I'm sorry she's making you go with me."

Sofie had been roped into this, too. The only thing she was getting out of it was the satisfaction of helping a friend. The realization kind of made Austin feel like a jerk. "*I'm* sorry," he said. "I agreed to go, and I'll be a good sport." He tossed the tie aside and waited for Amber to appear with a green paisley one.

"Dad's ties are all ugly, too," she said as she handed it to him. "But this is a little better than yours."

"I'm right here." Doug Waits waved at his daughter.

It took her a moment to realize she'd insulted his ties. "Sorry, Dad," she said.

A few more pictures were taken once Austin was ready. Sofie promised his mom that she'd get at least one picture of Amber with her date. Then the three of them left to pick up Amber's date.

****

Sofie oscillated between wanting to pinch herself and wanting to smack herself upside the head. She was on her way to the prom with a guy she was completely nuts about, and he had been bribed into going. This was not a smart idea.

While it was true that she was around Austin all the time and always managed to cover her lovesickness, he didn't always wear a suit and he didn't always smell like something spicy that she wanted to bury her nose in. It was going to take a lot of concentration to remember that Austin would not date his sister's friend and Amber would never forgive Sofie just for wishing that wasn't a fact.

Austin stopped the car in front of a house with beige sides and a brick front. Amber climbed out of the backseat then tapped on Sofie's window. "Come with me," she said.

Sofie followed Amber to the front door. James answered, looking a bit sullen. A woman who must have been his mom appeared behind him and asked if she could get a picture.

He said, "No," and pretty nearly shut the door in her face.

The second half of the drive was quiet compared to the first, and the first had only heard a few sentences about which turns to take.

The four of them lined up outside the school to show their tickets. Austin looked down at Sofie. "You feel okay about going in with the guy in the ugly tie?"

She felt a smile tugging on her lips. She could do this. She could act naturally. She had to. Her friendship with Amber was at stake. "I helped wash your car to get you to wear that tie," she said.

"I think you two washed the driveway as much as my car."

"We washed the car and had fun."

Austin glanced at his sister ahead of them. "It wasn't supposed to be fun for Amber."

"Well, if you have fun tonight that might even things up."

"It'll never happen," he said. But his eyes were bright, almost suggesting he was already having fun.

The music was upbeat when they entered, and James quickly joined a few guys he knew on the dance floor. He didn't seem to care whether or not Amber followed him so she hung back with Sofie and Austin. They chatted to some head bobbing.

James returned to claim Amber for a slow song. She looked so tense that Sofie tried to send encouraging looks from the sidelines, but Amber didn't seem capable of seeing anything other than his chin.

Austin did not ask Sofie to dance any of the slow songs. She did not ask him either. Her heart could hardly stand the nearness of leaning in to talk over the music. She was reasonably sure she would faint if there was actual touching. He and Sofie and Amber did eventually get moving when the music was fast. And despite what Austin still insisted, Sofie believed he was enjoying himself.

It got very warm in the crowded room though. James had disappeared again and Amber went to the bathroom. Austin and Sofie decided to step outside to cool off. "You won't be cold?" he asked as he pushed the door open.

"It'll feel good," she said. "As long as we're only out for a minute."

Austin nodded and pointed ahead on the sidewalk. "If we walk around that bench and back, we'll probably get in about the same time Amber is looking for us."

"Okay." Sofie pushed her lips together against the smile trying to get out. It had gotten dark. Even though they were technically at school and definitely not on a date, there was something undeniably romantic about a nighttime stroll. It was foolish to let herself indulge the sensation, but Sofie couldn't fight it. Or didn't want to fight it. She was just happy walking next to Austin.

Neither of them talked on the way to the bench. There were other kids milling about, most of them likely escaping the heat for a moment as well. Laughter drifted on the cool breeze and someone shouted something in the distance. They walked close enough to two guys to hear a snippet of their conversation.

One said, "How's your date?"

The other said, "I should never have asked her. She's totally boring and I won't even get to try anything because she had to have her brother drive us."

This was not a terribly shocking thing for a teenage boy to say. Sofie was still a little shocked because it was Amber's date who said it.

James turned to see who was nearby. The trace of surprise on his face was quickly replaced by defiance. He would not apologize and simply waited to see what Austin would say or do.

As the moment got tense, Sofie instinctively took a step backward.

Austin said, "I'm going to tell Amber that you had to go home because you got sick and if you don't leave now, you will feel sick."

James stood his ground, sizing up Austin and his threat. James had a little more bulk, but Austin was four or five inches taller and four or five inches angrier.

It was James' friend who spoke next. "Come on, man. Let's just go."

James kept his eyes on Austin but said, "You're right. This is a waste of time anyway." Then he turned to his friend, and they began to walk towards the parking lot.

Austin muttered something that sounded like, "Good riddance." He watched them leave before he turned to Sofie. "Don't tell Amber what really happened," he said. "We're going to say we found James out here puking."

"All right."

"I mean don't tell her next week either."

"I won't tell her." Sofie shook her head earnestly. "I'll only ever tell her that James is a pukeface."

Austin shook off the tension and motioned for her to continue their walk back inside. They delivered both versions of the message to Amber. All three of them had an even better time after that. They danced and laughed and left about fifteen minutes early to beat the rush out of the parking lot.

Sofie sat in the back with Amber to recount a few highlights of the night. A pair of guys had come up together to ask them to dance after James left. If Amber had any negative feelings about his early departure, that dance erased them. A girl they thought was a junior had at one point displayed some ballet moves to a song they were pretty sure no one had ever danced ballet to before. The girls were impressed and jealous.

Neither Sofie nor Amber was paying attention to where they were going so when they felt Austin put the car in park, Amber looked up and exclaimed, "Austin, you forgot to take Sofie home."

He turned to face the backseat. "You said she was going to stay the night with you."

"Oh, uh…" Amber bit her lip. "Maybe I forgot to tell you. I wanted her to stay, but her parents said she had to come straight home."

Austin sighed and started the car again.

"Wait," Amber said. "I'm going to get out while we're here. 'Night, Sofie." She opened the door and jumped out without waiting for Austin's permission.

He looked back at Sofie. "You want to move to the front?"

"All right." She jumped out, too, and waved to Amber as her friend looked back from her porch steps.

Austin's jacket and tie were in the passenger seat and he picked them up and threw them into the backseat to make room for Sofie. She asked him on the way to her house whether he thought he or Amber ended up with a better deal. He wouldn't admit he had fun, only that he got a better deal because he was a better negotiator.

When they stopped in front of her house, Sofie couldn't resist another question that was on her mind. "Austin, can I ask you something?" she said.

"Uh... yeah?" He sounded as though he'd picked up on her tone shift.

"Okay, maybe two things," she said. "First... were you bluffing when you threatened to hurt James tonight?"

"Mostly. He's not worth the trouble I'd have been in, but if he had swung first..."

"Also... um... when you asked me not to tell Amber what really happened with James, I thought you didn't want her to know you defended her because you two like to act like you can't stand each other. But I think maybe you were just as worried about her finding out what *he* said. Am I right?"

His crooked smile looked about as self-conscious as Sofie had ever seen him. He recovered quickly though and said, "I think I'll take the Fifth on that."

"Well, I think it was sweet," Sofie said. Then she leaned over and kissed him. On the cheek. Which. Did not. Make it any better. It was as though her brain had taken a sudden vacation and packed up all her common sense with it.

She felt her face heat up while she tried to decide if it would be less embarrassing to apologize for the lapse in judgment or pretend it didn't happen. She didn't have time to decide before Austin kissed her back. *Not* on the cheek.

He brushed her lips softly several times until Sofie felt her chest swell with so much emotion she didn't know what to do with it. She pulled away, said, "Goodnight," and flew out of the car. At least, she hoped she said goodnight. Her mouth was so preoccupied with remembering the touch that she couldn't be sure she got it to form the word.

She opened her front door and found her parents waiting up for her. Her mom was working on a crossword puzzle, and her dad appeared to have been startled awake by the sound of her coming home.

"How was it?" her mom asked.

Sofie only nodded. Words were still a little out of reach. The goodnight was implied as she raced down the hall to her bedroom. She closed the door and sat on her bed, not sure what to do or even what to think.

A light knock hit the door as her mom called out her name. When Sofie didn't answer, the door opened enough for her mom's head to poke inside. "Sofie?" she asked. "Are you all right?"

Sofie still didn't say anything, but her mouth sprang to life as a huge smile spread across it.

Angie Ennemoser smiled back as though she understood. "Goodnight, Sofie," she said as she closed the door.

Eventually, the pretty prom dress needed to come off. As Sofie changed into her pajamas, the euphoria of those last moments with Austin began to fade. Weak euphoria felt a lot like panic.

What was going to happen now? She couldn't tell Amber. Amber would flip out. Austin was likely flipping out already, regretting his own lapse in judgment. He didn't really... There was no way he actually... She couldn't possibly look him in the eye ever again. Not ever.

11 Present

A mber met her at the door with a plastic lei in each hand. "Which one do you want?" she asked.

"Um…" Sofie thought it was a difficult question only because she hadn't expected a question. She expected hi.

"Too slow," Amber said. "You get both." She threw the leis over Sofie's head one after the other.

"All right. Why are we wearing leis?"

Amber had one around her neck as well. "Because I promised my dad an *event*. I have no idea what is traditionally associated with croquet so I'm making things up." She tapped her orange and yellow lei. "These were cheap."

"They're summery anyway," Sofie said. "My parents are right behind me. You'll love the cake." Her mom had drawn croquet mallets with frosting and used candy pieces for wickets and balls.

Sofie left Amber with the greeting duty and walked through the house to the backyard to say hello to Amber's parents. Strings of blue and white lights had been hung along the fence. Music was playing, lawn chairs were lined up at the back of the house, and there was a large cooler of drinks on the deck. She found Joe studying a large sheet of paper taped to a window. "What's up, José?"

"Sofie," he said with a nod. "I'm just checking out the brackets here. Looks like you'll be playing Charlene first."

"Charlene? That still sounds weird to me." Amber's parents and Sofie's parents were trying to get everyone to use first names now that they were all adults. But Sofie had known her so long as Mrs. Waits that Charlene didn't exactly roll off her tongue.

"I don't mind the first names," Joe said with a shrug. "I'm just glad they're not trying to get me to call them Mom and Dad."

Sofie offered a look of agreement and tried not to think of a situation that might authorize her to call them Mom and Dad. She looked at the brackets, too. "Are we only playing two at a time?"

"Yep. Head-to-head, double elimination." Joe looked over his shoulder to make sure no one else was around and then turned back with a worried expression. "I think we might be here all night."

"It'll be fun," she said. She wanted to tell him he was wrong, but he probably wasn't. "Who do you play first?"

"Amber. She's been trash-talking since yesterday."

Sofie laughed. "What exactly does croquet trash-talking sound like?"

"It looks something like this." He pulled his phone from his pocket and showed Sofie the last two texts from Amber.

    I'm going to knock your ball so far off course
    the wicket will be in another zip code.

    I own the wickets and I will own you!

They were still laughing over the texts when Ken and Angie Ennemoser came outside. Sofie brought Joe over to appreciate the cake. Austin was behind Sofie's parents, helping his grandmother through the back door. They were all wearing leis, but Sofie was still the only one with two. Austin noticed.

"Why do you get two?" He gestured to her flowers. One strand was purple and yellow, the other was purple and green.

"Amber said I didn't choose fast enough. I guess you did." She eyed Austin's pink and red lei. It was mostly pink.

"Amber chose for me. She did all right though. I am totally rocking the pink."

Sofie laughed with him as the older Mrs. Waits observed, seemingly to no one in particular, "Someone who can make you laugh is a treasure."

"How are you today, Mrs. Waits?" Sofie asked, her face perfectly straight again.

"Better. I tweaked my wrist a few days ago pulling weeds, but it's better so I can play."

"Good. I didn't see who you'll be up against first."

"It's no matter," she said. "I'll be happy if I can see you and my grandson paired up."

"I... uh... I'm out of practice but I think I'll advance enough for that to happen."

The woman smiled at Sofie and then fixed her eyes solidly on Austin as she said, "I wasn't talking about croquet."

Sofie did and did not want to see Austin's reaction to that statement. She warred with herself for two agonizing seconds before Amber's voice came from behind her. "We're all here now."

Having an excuse to turn around, Sofie tried to see how annoyed Austin was by his grandmother. Rather than revealing anything himself, he seemed to be looking back at her for a reaction. The heat rushing to her cheeks would only get worse if she kept looking at him. She stepped forward to welcome Mr. Turner, who Amber had brought out as the last guest.

Doug Waits clapped his hands to get everyone's attention. His brown hair had picked up more specks of gray in the last few years. It looked like highlights in the sun. Amber hadn't exaggerated his excitement about the tournament. He bounced on his heels as he explained the rules and practically hopped when he showed off the fake gold trophies Amber had procured for the winner and runner-up. "Joe and Amber will start us off," he said with a big smile at his daughter, "whenever they are ready."

Amber picked up the red mallet and held it over her head like she was swinging a sledgehammer. "I was born ready."

Several people laughed or cheered or both. Austin calmly said, "Take her down, Joe."

Amber sneered at her brother. "I don't need you. I already have plenty of people on my side."

"They only want you to win," he said, "because they know you'll be easier to beat."

"We'll see." She handed a mallet to Joe while her dad tossed a coin to see who would go first. Joe beat her soundly, and no one was surprised. Amber wasn't very competitive. She only talked big to try to get everyone else into the spirit of the event. It seemed to work, though it was possible everyone simply arrived in good moods. They happily shared the cake and the drinks. They laughed at the wayward shots and cheered the victors no matter who they were.

A few rounds in, Sofie's mom was playing Austin's grandmother and Austin was assisting. He was alternating between holding her cane, her mallet and her arm. She was intentionally making it difficult for him to know which to take next. They both enjoyed the confusion as much as the spectators did.

A slower song began to play and Doug Waits held his arm out to his wife. "Would you care to dance?" he said.

She smiled and rose from her chair to join him.

"What a splendid idea," Mr. Turner said. He came over to Sofie and bowed. "Would you do me the honor, Sofie my dear?"

She was amused by his overly polite demeanor and said, "I'd be delighted."

He twirled her around on their way to join the other dancers. "I believe we last danced at your parents' 20th anniversary party," he said.

"I believe you tried to teach me a waltz, and I nearly broke your ankle."

"You young people remember way too much. I only remember that we danced."

Sofie smiled, thinking that she didn't remember enough. She had to concentrate to keep up with what he called a simple step. Once she felt as though she had the rhythm down, she tried to talk again. "Have I convinced you not to retire yet?"

"I'm afraid I'm as stubborn as you are."

"Have I at least talked you into staying in town?"

He smiled. "And let my new toy go to waste?"

"You've proven you can camp locally."

"True. I will only be gone temporarily though." As he looked at Sofie, the lines around his eyes seemed to soften. "I have decided to visit my brother."

"Really? Have you been in touch with him then?" Sofie hoped it was okay to ask since he brought it up. Mr. Turner had one brother he rarely mentioned. She knew they'd been estranged for nearly thirty years, but he'd never talked about the reason or reasons why.

The older man nodded solemnly. "There's been no official reconciliation. I mentioned that I would be in his neck of the woods and he confirmed his address. I suppose that's enough. I find as I get older that I have less need for apology and more need for family."

"We're your family," Sofie said.

"Yes, dear." He smiled. "But one can always have more and I think… it is possible after some time away I will decide retirement doesn't suit me so well after all."

"I hope so. I hear you need to be at least sixty to retire anyway."

"True." He nodded thoughtfully. He'd blown out fifty-nine candles all eight birthdays he'd celebrated at the bakery. They danced quietly for a minute as he tried to change the step to match a new song. "I have to admit it feels good."

"What does?" Sofie asked, assuming he didn't mean her tromping on his toes.

"It has been a very long time since I've had a young man jealous of me."

"What are you talking about?"

"Austin," he said. His eyes twinkled with amusement.

"What do you mean?"

Mr. Turner smiled over her shoulder. "He's watching us, watching *you*. And if I'm not mistaken, he'd very much like to take my place."

"I suspect he's only growing tired of juggling canes." Sofie refused to look back and see that her old friend was wrong.

"Perhaps," he said. He spun Sofie around. "Or perhaps he's watching because we are such fabulous dancers."

She laughed at that because she nearly tripped over her own foot trying to get back into position. They had to quit the dance anyway because it turned out that Austin was looking at Sofie because it was her turn to play. She faced Joe in her second game and beat him easily.

Joe was right about it being a long night. Austin's grandmother went home as soon as she was eliminated. Mr. Turner and Sofie's parents left not long afterwards. Sofie was playing Austin for the chance to meet his dad in the championship match. Austin was using yellow because Sofie had used it in her last match and said it must be her lucky color.

"I still can't believe you stole my color," she said to him as he was about to line up a shot.

"You wouldn't want to win on luck, would you?"

"I think I need the advantage."

Austin pointed to her red ball. "You're ahead."

"Oh, look at that. I am ahead." Sofie acted as though she just noticed that.

Austin very maturely stuck his tongue out at her.

He pulled ahead of her after a few more turns though, then got a chance to knock her ball into "the badlands." That's what they'd nicknamed a certain area of the yard when they were kids. It had many knobby tree roots sticking up through the grass.

"Boo!" Amber called from the sidelines. "Austin gets a technical foul for unsportsmanlike conduct."

"God put the roots there," Austin said.

"No problem," Doug said. "Sofie can handle herself in the badlands."

Sofie gave him a thumbs up for the support and looked at Austin. "How does it feel to have your entire family rooting against you?"

"They are not," Austin protested. "Mom's on my side. Right, Mom?"

Charlene held her hands out in an apologetic gesture. "Sorry, honey. If only you'd stop giving me funny looks about my hair."

Austin hung his head in feigned disappointment. Sofie was having a lot of fun. If only she could limit her time with Austin to crowds, things might actually go back to normal. She made a Hail Mary shot through the tree roots, and it almost paid off.

They both soon had possible winning shots lined up. But it was Austin's turn.

She tried to taunt him. "You'll never make that."

"You might as well give up now, Austin." Amber had come closer to examine the situation. "I've seen you miss far easier shots."

"Thanks for that vote of confidence. Now go back to the stands."

Amber laughed at him calling the mismatched group of lawn chairs stands.

Sofie said, "Shh! He needs to concentrate."

Austin put his mallet to the ground as he turned his back on both of them. Sofie was sure he didn't want them to know he thought they were funny. He tapped the yellow ball, and it glanced off the outside of the wicket. Everyone who claimed to be rooting against him groaned.

Sofie quickly got her ball through the wicket to much cheering. She noticed as Austin congratulated her that he didn't appear all that disappointed. That triggered an unwelcome thought. "You didn't just let me win, did you?"

"No." He shook his head and seemed surprised by the accusation.

"Are you sure?"

"I really couldn't help it," he said. "You're… distracting."

The way he said it made Sofie think he wasn't talking about her heckling. She quickly turned to face her next competitor before her mind could let her imagine Austin flirting with her. He wouldn't do that. She'd been clear that making fun of her declaration was off the table and while Austin did have some faults, being intentionally hurtful was not one of them. If only she could convince her own mind to stop torturing her with possibilities that were not possibilities.

12 PAST

Without some form of the red suit, he was just a fat man with a beard. Austin waved his hand in front of the display to watch what was supposed to be a vacationing Santa stretch and yawn again. His dad might get a kick out of it. The others would think it was lame, and rightfully so.

Austin moved down the aisle. He was beginning to think the Christmas section would not be the best place to find a present. He checked his watch. The time was, "Hurry up, you procrastinating moron!"

It was Christmas Eve and Austin was going to a Dirty Santa party at Sofie's house. Her parents and his had become nearly as tight as Sofie and Amber. Austin felt like an outsider and knew he'd been invited out of obligation. He had planned to skip the party until his mom informed him that was not an option. He was not allowed to "snub" the Ennemosers any more than he was allowed to be by himself on Christmas Eve.

A part of him did want to go to the party anyway, the not insignificant part of him that wanted to see Sofie. He hadn't seen her since he'd been home for Christmas Break. He'd actually seen very little of her since the night of the prom. Amber had suddenly spent all her time at Sofie's house instead of the way it had been before the prom. And Sofie ducked away if he got a passing glimpse of her at school. He kissed her and she ran away and disappeared on him. The message was that she was not interested in dating the guy who called her a name she hated and laughed at her taste in cereal and once pelted her with water balloons on a dare from Dillon.

It had been months though. Maybe he wasn't that guy anymore. Or maybe she could eventually grow to like that guy.

If she wasn't still freaked out about him stealing a premature kiss.

Austin had wandered into a section of towels and bedding while thinking about Sofie. Nothing there would work for the party. He made an abrupt right and found himself facing a jewelry counter. No. As he turned again though, a stand of crystal bracelets caught his eye. He reached out and fingered some purple beads as he remembered similar beads scattered across the carpet. He'd once broken a bracelet somewhat like this one during a skirmish with his sister.

Amber had yelled at him that it was Sofie's bracelet while she tried to gather all the beads. She wasn't able to put it back together and eventually admitted – when pressed by their mom – that it breaking was as much her fault as it was Austin's. Sofie had never mentioned the loss. Did she care about the bracelet? Would she appreciate him trying to replace it years later or not even remember it?

Those were questions he couldn't answer and didn't have time to ponder. He moved to a section of winter hats and grabbed a fairly ridiculous one with ear flaps and a giant wad of yarn sticking out the top. If he couldn't find a good gift, bad on purpose was the next best thing.

Amber was ready to pounce when he got back to the house. "It's about time," she said. "We're going to be late because of you."

"No, we're not," he insisted, even though they were running a little behind. He searched the house for wrapping paper and did a hasty, tape-heavy job covering the hat.

Amber sneered at it as the family left and said, "That is the ugliest present I have ever seen."

"Don't worry, it's ugly on the inside, too."

She looked annoyed that she hadn't annoyed him. "At least the poor wrapping will make yours obvious so no one will pick it by mistake."

He shrugged.

Their mom said, "Just get in the car, you two." There wasn't a ton of Christmas spirit in her voice at that moment, but she summoned it by the time Mrs. Ennemoser greeted them at her door.

The moms blew air kisses at each other while the dads did a combination handshake and hug. Amber ran off to "find Sofie" and Austin took a seat next to Mr. Turner. He'd only met the older man once before but thought they could commiserate over their outlier status. This consisted of small talk about school, the bakery and the delicious smells of the impending dinner.

Austin's parents remained standing in the front hall chatting excitedly with Sofie's parents as though they hadn't just seen each other a week ago. Their voices eventually drifted towards the kitchen. The house was only vaguely familiar to Austin. He'd eaten dinner there once before and stopped in a few times when he'd been coerced into driving Amber and Sofie somewhere.

He'd never been there with the Christmas decorations up. The tree was bright. It appeared to have more lights than ornaments. Draped across one wall was a string of white circles about the size of dessert plates. Each one showed a picture of a Christmas tree signed by Sofie. On the first one, her name was written with a backwards S and the spikey tree had only two large ornaments. The pictures got progressively better and became very good only halfway through. The tree that must have been done for the current year was practically glowing. She'd used some sort of neon pens on the ornaments and the edge of the branches.

Mrs. Ennemoser invited Austin and Mr. Turner to the table before she moved down the hall to "find the girls." Sofie, evidently, made a habit of getting lost.

Eight people were going to be a tight squeeze around the table. Austin was to sit in the middle of one side, between his dad and Mr. Turner. They asked him to sit first so they could push their chairs in. He was feeling a bit trapped when Sofie entered the room, followed by Amber. Sofie was wearing a pretty red dress with a necklace of tiny candy canes. The table seemed to be holding Austin back and not keeping him far enough away at the same time.

Sofie smiled over her shoulder at Amber and appeared to be making her way to the center chair on the opposite side until her eyes fell on Austin. Her smile faltered, and she dropped her gaze to her hands. She quickly pushed herself against the table to make a path for Amber to claim that middle seat instead.

Amber noticed Austin across from her as she sat, and she wrinkled up her nose as though detecting a bad odor. It was not a surprise that Amber thought facing Austin was distasteful, but it stung that Sofie apparently found it even more so. She carefully kept her eyes on her half of the table while she situated herself in her chair.

Perhaps Austin was wrong though. Pink had bloomed across Sofie's cheeks. He could feel that his own ears were warm. Was there any chance she was flushing for the same reason? Had his absence made her heart grow fonder? Or was she just mad at him about the kiss?

He tried to watch her covertly during the meal. It seemed she was doing the same thing, constantly turning away if he caught her looking. Her lips twitched against a smile that was adorable half the time. The other half he wasn't so sure because he couldn't figure out if she was enjoying the eye banter or laughing at him.

He needed to know and began searching for an opportunity to ask as they all worked to clear the table. At first, talking to Sofie alone seemed impossible. Eight people fully filled the space between the kitchen and dining room, and Amber was moving with Sofie like they were conjoined twins.

And then something of a miracle occurred. As Austin followed the girls into the dining room, Amber said, "Oh, I heard my name. I think the moms are talking about me," and she ran from the room to either defend herself or bask in the praise.

Mr. Ennemoser called Mr. Turner back to the kitchen for some reason and Austin didn't know where anyone else was. He only knew that he was unexpectedly standing in the dining room with Sofie and no one else.

"Sofie," he whispered.

She had picked up a few napkins and she brought them closer to hear him. She stared at him with anticipation as Austin realized he hadn't decided what to say. He likely had less than a minute to find out if she was angry about what happened between them or simply unsure or if it meant nothing or… "Do I, um… do I need to apologize?"

"For…?" Her lovely blue eyes ran over his face and the way they stuttered at his mouth told him that she knew what he was talking about. Slowly, she began to move her head side to side.

Austin felt a weight lift. She hadn't minded so much then?

He was about to tell her he was glad because he wasn't the least bit sorry when she said, "I understand."

She understood? If there was something to understand, she was going to have to explain it to him. Before he could ask what she meant though, she said, "Amber would have had a fit anyway," as she nearly ran out of the room with those napkins.

Then Austin did understand. He understood *anyway*. Amber would have had a fit *anyway*. As in, even if Sofie didn't still think of him like an annoying brother, Amber would have been a problem.

****

Sofie closed the door and leaned her back against it. She didn't need a bathroom. She needed a minute where no one could see her face.

How could she be so shocked by something that wasn't a surprise? She already knew Austin never really meant to kiss her. Having him confirm it with an apology should have affected her little, if at all. It was hope's fault. She'd let hope sneak up on her during dinner. Austin asked her to pass a dish, and he took it with an expression she imagined held something special for her. It was only her imagination and she'd let it infect her with hope anyway. For the first time since she'd doodled his name in her 6th grade notebook, she'd dared to believe Austin might see her as an actual girl and not just his sister's friend.

Even fleeting hope fell hard. Sofie could handle it though. She might be out of practice since Austin had been away at school a few months, but she could go back to her family room and have a Christmas party as though there wasn't someone nearby who made her pulse race. Sofie stepped in front of the sink and peered into the mirror. She practiced smiling until it felt natural and whispered Austin's name until she could say it with that hint of irritation Amber always had.

Her mom was handing around a bowl of numbers when Sofie walked into the family room. "Just you and me," she said as she held the bowl out.

Sofie saw two folded slips of paper and plucked one of them. Number eight. She'd be the last one to choose a present.

"Bring in the cookies, please." Angie Ennemoser handed Sofie the bowl while she unfolded the last number for herself.

Sofie swapped the empty bowl for a tray of cookies she knew were wonderful because she helped make them. She had sampled several. She placed the cookies on the coffee table and placed herself on the floor next to Amber.

"What number are you?" Amber whispered.

Sofie showed Amber her paper. Amber held out her number – a two – and Sofie nodded at it.

"Who's going to start us off?" Ken Ennemoser asked as he welcomed his wife onto the sofa next to him.

Charlene Waits stood and waved her slip of paper. "Looks like I have that honor." She examined the presents under the tree and then winked at Austin as she selected an oddly shaped and badly wrapped package.

"You know she's only picking yours out of pity, right?" Amber was looking sadly at her brother.

He shrugged innocently. "What makes you think that one's mine?"

She just rolled her eyes in response.

Mrs. Waits returned to her seat. She opened the present and laughed. "I love it," she said. And she may have been serious. She put the hat on her head and used her hand to fluff up the blue yarn on top. She grinned with satisfaction and said, "Who's next?"

Amber jumped up and went to the tree. Her hands closed around a box covered with fancy warnings. Scripty letters spelled out things like "This end up," "Do not shake" and "Fragile."

"I'm so curious about this one I can't stand it," Amber said. She took it carefully back to her spot on the carpet and began to peel off the paper.

Sofie's eagerness grew as Amber gently unwrapped the box because she knew Amber was going to like it. She'd caught a glimpse of her mom working on them.

Amber slowly lifted the lid to reveal four cupcakes. Each one was decorated with a nativity silhouette surrounded by icing scrollwork. Amber – and several other people – exclaimed at the beauty of the treats. Then Amber sucked in a surprised breath, tilted her head to see the cupcakes from the side, and lifted her eyes to question Mrs. Ennemoser. "These are carrot cake, aren't they?" Her tone was awed.

Sofie's mom smiled and nodded.

Amber slowly closed the lid on the box and slid it protectively behind her, which made laughter fill the room.

After it died down, Austin said, "I hate to be the bearer of bad news but..."

Amber's mouth dropped open.

"... I have number three," he finished, staring pointedly behind Amber.

"You wouldn't!" she said.

He pretended to think about it before he said, "Hand them over."

Amber sort of crumpled on the floor before she got up and grudgingly placed the box of cupcakes in Austin's hands. He lifted the lid for a peek and nodded approvingly.

An idea came out of nowhere and slapped a mischievous grin onto Amber's face. "In that case," she said, "I'm going to take your dumb hat just so Mom will steal the cupcakes from you." She snatched the hat from her mom's head and returned to her seat wearing the hat and a satisfied expression.

Everyone in the room – except for Sofie – turned to Mrs. Waits to see what she would do. Sofie sort of looked at Mrs. Waits and sort of looked at the floppy hat that was now next to her. She was glad Amber had taken it. Sofie wanted the hat, but she didn't want anyone to guess why she wanted the hat. Maybe if Amber ended up with it, she'd give it to Sofie.

Mrs. Waits sighed and cast a longing look at the box Austin was holding.

"You would steal from your own child," he deadpanned. "On Christmas."

"It's Christmas *Eve*," Amber corrected. "Don't let him guilt you, Mom."

"I'll bet there are a lot of good presents." Mrs. Waits sent Amber an apologetic glance as she reached under the tree. She ripped off the shiny red paper to reveal a container of chocolate covered almonds. "I was right," she said.

"Those look delicious," Mr. Turner said. He leaned from his chair to take the almonds without getting up. "And I think someone here knows they are my favorite." He winked at Sofie. "Thank you, my dear."

She accepted his gratitude with a demure smile. They all knew who had brought which present, but she knew she wasn't supposed to acknowledge it.

"I think I'm going to have to take those cupcakes now."

Amber cheered as her mom relieved Austin of the precious package.

"That's okay," he said as he went to claim a new present. "Mom's going to share with me anyway."

Amber opened her mouth in what was surely going to be a protest. Then her face shifted hopefully and she said, "There are four of them."

Mrs. Waits closed the box she'd been examining. "You kids will have to get your own cupcakes. These look almost too good to eat."

Austin, meanwhile, had unwrapped a book of pocket proverbs. He flipped through the pages and said, "I like the one about the dog eating his own vomit."

"You would," Amber said, while a few others laughed.

His mom sighed.

Mr. Turner said, "Something for everyone in there I think."

Sofie's mom looked around the room and asked what number they were on. Mr. Turner pointed out that he was the last to choose and his number was four.

"That makes it my turn," Ken Ennemoser said. He smiled at Amber's dad. "Clearly Doug and I were thinking alike so I'll take his present."

Under the tree were two similarly shaped gifts that, though wrapped, were still identifiable as six-packs of beer. Mr.

Ennemoser picked up one of those and tore off the paper before he held it on his lap.

His wife tsked in the seat next to him. "I can't believe you brought alcohol to an exchange that includes minors."

"Why wouldn't I?" he asked. "It only increases the odds I'll end up with it."

She shook her head at him.

"Let me help." Doug Waits grabbed two cookies from the center of the room on his way to retrieve the beer that had just been unwrapped. "I wouldn't want you to be in trouble with the wife or anything. I'll just take this off your hands."

"Thanks." Sofie's dad stressed the word with sarcasm and then eyed his wife as though he was actually afraid of her. "I guess I can't just grab that other one then?"

"Do what you like." She tried to make her voice disapproving but ruined it with a smile. They both knew she wasn't really mad.

Mr. Ennemoser played along by picking out a different gift. He opened a vanilla scented candle on a glass stand. There wasn't time to read his reaction before his wife seized it. "I like this," she said. "And it's my turn."

He grinned and took the beer back from his friend.

Mr. Waits took the cupcakes from his wife, who looked shocked only for a moment before she reclaimed the hat from Amber. Amber jumped up to get the cupcakes from her dad. He took the beer again.

Mr. Ennemoser sighed and took the last present that wasn't beer. He opened a box that contained many small spools of Christmas ribbon.

"I thought—" Amber cut herself off. "I mean, someone probably thought at least one person here would still have presents to wrap." Her eyes pointed at Austin with a suggestion that he try to deny it.

"Was that person under the impression that I got you something?" he asked.

Amber narrowed her eyes at her brother, clearly thinking of a comeback.

Their mom looked at Sofie's mom. "It must be so peaceful at your house when we're not here."

Sofie decided to take her turn. Peaceful was nice, but she liked having the Waitses around, too. All of them. "My presents are wrapped," she said, "but I think this ribbon will come in handy next year." Sofie sent an appreciative glance at Amber as she took the box from her dad.

He stepped across the room with a triumphant laugh as he claimed the beer yet again, which set off a massive flurry of gift-grabbing. Mr. Waits took the chocolate almonds from Mr. Turner, who apologized profusely to Amber as he took the cupcakes from her. Then Amber took the ribbon from Sofie and she took the cupcakes from Mr. Turner so he could get the almonds back from Amber's dad. Mr. Waits shook his head as though he was at a loss for what to do. Then he took the hat from his wife's head. She announced that Amber could not keep her own gift as she took the ribbon from her. Amber happily reclaimed the cupcakes from Sofie, who grabbed the candle from her mom. Mrs. Ennemoser said that if taking your own gift wasn't against the rules, she might as well enjoy her handiwork.

Amber pouted as the cupcakes left her possession again. Then she turned and took the candle from Sofie. Sofie took the ribbon back from Amber's mom, who took the hat back from her husband. He took the chance to take the beer again, which caused Mr. Ennemoser to gently remove the cupcakes from his wife's hands with a promise that they could share them.

She laughed and took the hat as though it didn't matter what she had as long as she didn't open the last present. Mrs. Waits took the ribbon from Sofie, who took the cupcakes from her dad with a conspiratorial nod to Amber. Mr. Ennemoser moved the hat from his wife's head to his. She looked around the room with a sly grin and made a move towards Austin.

Sofie had been watching him. One side of his mouth was lifted in a smile that said he was very aware of the happy chaos going on around him. The other side appeared more studious, as he was reading the proverbs at the same time.

His eyes came up laughing as Sofie's mom yanked the book out from under them. He smiled as he pointed thoughtfully to the various gifts around the room. Sofie could hear the words he teased her with when he wasn't even saying them. She also knew the decision he'd made before his dark blue eyes found her and the cupcakes in front of her. Heaven have mercy if he ever looked at her the way he looked at those cupcakes.

He said nothing as he walked closer to retrieve them. Sofie caught the familiar scent of him as he bent to pick up the box. When he said, "Thank you," it sounded like provocation for revenge. She didn't care. She could get exactly what she wanted.

"I know how to end this," she said, "because I know who really wants that last gift." She pulled the hat from her dad's head.

He stood. "If you insist," he said as he grabbed the last present from under the tree.

Sofie pulled the silly hat onto her head and faced Amber, who cracked up at the sight of her. Perfect. Sofie could wear the hat all winter just to make her friend laugh. Well, maybe not *just* to make Amber laugh. And perhaps wearing a reminder on her head was not going to be the best way to forget Amber had a brother. Even so… the hat felt like a perfect fit.

13 PRESENT

H e didn't want to feel guilty. He'd just spent the previous evening as her personal croquet assistant. There was still a little jab of guilt when Austin carefully avoided his grandmother at church. She always sat in the front left so he found a seat in the back right, which was not coincidentally a good place to see who was coming in. Sofie was either running late or not coming.

Austin kept his grandmother in his sight as he made his way out of the church. He was prepared to wave if she saw him, but she didn't. He moved ahead of her to the parish hall for a donut. Then he helped himself to another one. He was too restless to sit around so he filled a cup with water and stepped outside again.

He crossed paths with Monsignor Loy on the sidewalk. "Good morning, my sheep." The priest smiled and smoothed his beard. "Are you alone today?"

"Looks that way," Austin said.

"Physically but not spiritually, of course."

"Of course." Austin nodded at the correction that was not insignificant. He was trying to rely on God to find a time to talk to Sofie. The reminder helped. It was harder to be impatient with God than with Sofie.

"I hear there's a bug going around," Monsignor Loy said. "I hope that isn't the reason you're without family."

"No. They were all fine last night. I'm sure they're just coming later."

"Good, good." He nodded and moved towards the parish hall before he turned back to Austin. "You might be surprised how often you've been coming up when I talk to your sister."

"Uh…" Austin had no idea what to say to that.

The man in black didn't appear to expect him to say anything. He just smiled again and continued into the hall.

Austin paced up and down the sidewalk, trying to decide what to do with himself. He wanted to talk to Sofie in person but waiting outside the church two weeks in a row might qualify as harassment if she didn't want him to be anything to her beyond her friend's brother. But how was he supposed to know what she wanted if she refused to talk to him? The impatience was creeping back already.

He couldn't ask her out over the phone because it was too easy for her to hang up. He didn't even know why she thought it was a joke so he'd never figure out how to explain it wasn't before she pushed a button. He couldn't write a letter detailing his feelings because... well, because he was a guy. Plus, he'd have no way of knowing if she actually read it. Talking to her in person seemed like the only way to make progress. Even though it hadn't exactly gone over well last time and even though he still didn't know what he'd done wrong then. Sofie was an amazing puzzle but a puzzle no less.

"Austin!"

His thoughts were interrupted by a female voice calling to him from the nearby parking lot. The voice, unfortunately, belonged to his sister. Austin tossed his cup into a trash can as he waited for her anyway.

"Sofie's got me hooked on church coffee now," she said as she reached him. "What's your excuse?"

"For being here? It's called Sunday."

"You know I meant why are you hanging around between masses?" Amber said. "I'm betting that it isn't coffee and that it has something to do with Sofie."

"We've only been out a minute." Austin motioned to a pair of older women chatting by the church exit. The man waiting for them was leaning against the wall with his eyes closed as though he'd been camped out for some time. The scene didn't back up his claim that he'd more or less just walked out.

Amber smirked knowingly. "I'll tell you what," she said. "I'm going to be very nice and invite you to sit with us so you can tell Sofie that I invited you to join us."

"I don't need an excuse," Austin said. It was easy to refuse Amber's offer because he couldn't talk to Sofie about what he wanted to talk about with Amber around and because he'd been refusing anything from his sister for so long it was pretty much a reflex.

Amber should have been used to it, but she got a strangely disappointed look on her face. "Oh, wait," she said. "Does Sofie know?"

"She knows you're here anyway." Austin nodded towards Sofie, who was headed towards them.

Amber took a quick glance and then faced Austin seriously. "Is she avoiding you because she *knows* you have a thing for her?"

"Stay out of it," he said.

Amber's frustrated brow meant that he hadn't answered her question. That was the good news. The bad news was that she gave no indication that she intended to stay out of it. "What did you do to make her so mad?" she hissed.

Austin refused to answer or even acknowledge the question.

Amber put on a fake cheerful face as Sofie got closer. "Sofie," she said, "look who I found. I was trying to convince him to come to coffee and donuts with us. Will you help me?"

"Help you... um... convince him?" Sofie looked between the siblings as though she suspected they were setting her up for a practical joke.

"I already had a donut so I—"

"You can have another," Amber said.

"I already had two actually."

Amber glared at him as though he wasn't helping because he *wasn't* helping. That amused Austin and seemed to convince Sofie that they were behaving normally. She said, "Bye, Austin," as she turned towards the parish hall. Amber gave him a gentle shove as she turned the same way.

Austin watched them for a moment, watched Sofie. When she looked over her shoulder at him, it was a much better invitation than any Amber had issued. He began to follow them.

Sofie's hair was braided. The end of it was tied with a tiny pink ribbon in the middle of her back. One of the ends of the bow hung longer than the other, tempting Austin to catch up enough to pull the ribbon out and let her hair loose the way it was more often. She would probably not thank him for that. Austin caught up enough to touch the ribbon but did not.

"Changed your mind?" Sofie asked as he walked into the parish hall with them.

"Two donuts make a person thirsty," he said. He ignored the gloating look on Amber's face. She took a cup to the coffee urn while Austin followed Sofie to the water fountain. "The early mass wasn't working for you?" he asked.

Sofie smiled. "If I told anyone else I wanted to sleep in because I was playing croquet until one in the morning, he wouldn't believe me."

"But you think I do? You gotta admit that sounds pretty far-fetched."

"I have a plastic trophy to prove it. Though I feel kind of bad about beating your dad."

"You shouldn't. He was more or less taking credit for your victory, saying he taught you how to play and all."

"You know, I heard you telling him it should be an annual event." Sofie eyed him with a suspicious smile. It looked like she was daring him to deny he'd enjoyed the long night.

Austin had enjoyed it, but he still had an honest defense. "Did you hear what he said before that?"

"No."

"He was talking about doing it again like in a few weeks. When I suggested annually, I was trying to space out the tournaments."

"Maybe that sounds far-fetched," Sofie said. She took her full cup away from the fountain and Austin caught up to her as she got to the table where Amber was sitting. Amber's cup was on the table and her face was sort of floating over it.

"You look nuts," Sofie said as she sat. Austin had been about to say exactly the same thing. No wonder he liked Sofie so much.

"Just because you don't like coffee." Amber included Austin as though she knew what he'd been thinking. "Everyone else here understands me."

"I doubt that."

Amber pretended not to hear Austin's words. She only looked at Sofie. "Did you finish the book last night?"

"I, uh…" Sofie sipped her water in an obvious attempt to delay her answer. "I fell asleep."

"You what!? How could you fall asleep? You were so near the end, and I read it in like two days because it was so good."

Austin thought about pointing out that Sofie had a job. Though it would simply be a statement of fact, Amber would find offense if Austin was the one who said it. She'd had a job lined up when she graduated, but the company went through "restructuring" that resulted in her and a few other recent hires being let go after she'd barely gotten started. For some reason, she seemed to take it as a personal rejection. He held his tongue to see what Sofie would say.

She gave a weak shrug. "I was tired. Remember how late it was when I left your house?"

"Yeah, I suppose last night wasn't great for reading. I'm just anxious for you to finish so we can talk about it. Aren't you dying to know…" Amber paused with her mouth still open and a sly expression flit across her face before she continued. "… what his next move will be?"

"His next…?" Sofie tilted her head. "You know I only have a chapter and a half left. He's already declared himself. I just need to find out how she reacts."

"So it's *her* turn to… say something."

"Yeah?" Sofie drew the word out into a question.

Austin had nearly checked out of the conversation when he realized they were talking about some mushy girl book. Amber's eyes pulled him back in though. They drifted towards him in a way that suggested she wasn't talking about a book at all.

"What does she need to tell him?" Amber asked.

"I'll find out soon."

Amber greedily inhaled steam from her cup. "What if it was you?"

"In the book?" Sofie laughed. "He's written as a nearly perfect match for her. Obviously, if I was in charge of the outcome, she'd accept him."

Amber nodded and she was nearly smirking at Austin. But Sofie was talking about a book and he wanted to keep it that way as long as Amber was around. He located his sister's toe under the table and pressed firmly with his shoe. She jerked away and glared at him, but she seemed to get his point.

She sighed and said, "I think I've talked Joe into joining us next week."

"If Joe comes, you won't need me."

"I still need you," Amber said. "Are you over the early mass though?"

"I... uh..." Sofie's eyes found Austin and then quickly looked away. "I haven't decided."

There was something in her glance that was less panicky than he expected. It almost looked as though she was deciding whether or not to keep avoiding him, rather than simply how to keep avoiding him. That might be an improvement. Unless of course he wasn't going to like what she said when they talked. It was best not to worry about that unless it happened. "Are you sticking around for lunch today?" he asked.

Austin was talking to Sofie, but Amber butted in with a poke on his arm. "Are you going to church twice?"

"I could," he said, "but I thought I'd run home for a bit and meet everyone at the restaurant."

"Except that you don't know where we're going. We are *not* doing The Sleepy Crab again because I cannot take that music another week."

"What's wrong with a little pirate music?" he asked innocently.

Sofie began to sing. "Hoist the anchor and away we go. Shiver me timbers and a yo ho ho." She smiled at Austin as he joined in with a very deep yo ho ho.

Amber looked as though she might be about to throw her hot coffee on the pair of them. She cradled it closer to her instead. "You two are not funny," she said.

"Have you been there without the rest of us," Austin asked Sofie, "because I'm surprised that line came to you so easily after several missed weeks."

"I have an excellent memory," she said. "Unfortunately." The last word she mumbled into her cup.

"So *are* you joining us for lunch this week?" Amber looked at Sofie when she asked the question but cast annoying shifty glances at Austin while waiting for an answer.

"I guess I will," Sofie said. "I need to eat."

Amber grinned and continued to look between Sofie and Austin as though she was plotting something.

It irritated Austin, and he decided it was best to leave before Sofie thought he had anything to do with whatever she might say next. "I'm going to go," he said. Sofie had one arm resting on the table. He touched it with his fingertips as he stood. "Text me which restaurant she talks everyone into, okay?"

Sofie nodded, but she also looked down at her arm as though she was bothered by the contact. Austin left trying to pretend he hadn't noticed that or his sister mouthing the words, "I knew you liked her," behind Sofie's back.

He passed a couple in the parking lot on his way to his car. He didn't know what was going on between them and didn't care, but he felt a slight pang of jealousy because the guy appeared to have the girl's rapt attention. His life would be a lot easier if he could get Sofie to stay in one place long enough to spell out exactly where he stood with her.

He made the short drive home with the windows down because the air conditioning wouldn't have time to cool off. The noise of rushing wind couldn't blow away the growing impatience. Neither could the sight of his empty apartment. He'd been there nearly two months and he hadn't finished unpacking. There were a few boxes in the middle of his living room that he hadn't felt like sorting through and nothing on the walls. It had simply seemed like there was no hurry to get his place organized.

Looking at the mess now, it suddenly gave the impression that he was waiting for something. Perhaps waiting for someone to give him incentive to get things organized or just waiting for someone to organize it for.

To convince himself that wasn't the case, Austin sat and opened one of the boxes. It had clothes on top, long-sleeved shirts he wouldn't need for months. He looked at his watch and then dug around in the box. He found nothing that begged to be put away and shoved the whole box aside in favor of another one.

He found a few pans, which was good because he thought he owned more than the two in the kitchen. The box also contained high school yearbooks. He opened his senior one and instinctively flipped to the prom page. There was a picture of Sofie and Amber dancing next to an arm he knew was his. Though Amber had been the one desperate to attend, Sofie looked thoroughly happy in the picture.

When a text came to Austin's phone with lunch plans, it came from his dad and not from Sofie. He was afraid that meant she wasn't going out to lunch after all. He was right. He wanted to wish he could interpret her general avoidance as easily. But the most obvious reason was that she didn't want to have to tell him she was no longer interested. He wasn't going to believe that unless she actually said it.

14 PAST

They were laughing out on the front porch. Austin closed the refrigerator and paced the kitchen. He wasn't hungry anyway, just impatient for Dillon to show up so they could head to the park. Another burst of laughter tempted him to go outside to wait for Dillon. Would Sofie see through that excuse and run away? Was it worth making a fool of himself to see her for a minute or two?

Hang on. That was Dillon's voice. Was he already here and making Sofie laugh while Austin was waiting for him inside? This was the first time they'd gotten together all summer and apparently Dillon had spent his second year of college becoming annoying.

The front door popped open and Amber's voice called out, "Dillon's here!" A moment later the door banged shut and Dillon appeared in the kitchen.

"Hey, man," he said. "Your sister let me in."

"I heard. You ready to go?"

Dillon jerked his head towards the door he'd entered. "Let's ask them to join us."

"They won't. Amber hates basketball."

"Hmm." Dillon frowned and then pulled himself up so that he was sitting on the counter behind him. "Do you want to do something else?"

"You mean something the girls will agree to?"

"It might be fun." His voice was nonchalant, but it was clear to Austin that Dillon wanted to change their plans because of his encounter on the porch.

"You still interested in Sofie?" he asked.

Dillon shrugged. "I don't know about still. I mean, it's probably been a year since I've seen her but…" He lowered his voice to a whisper. "She's even hotter than I remember."

Austin couldn't argue that point any more than he could argue against Dillon having become annoying. "Fine," he said. "Let's go talk to them."

His shoes hit the floor hard when Dillon pushed himself off the counter to follow Austin back out to the porch. Sofie and Amber were sitting in white rocking chairs. Sofie's legs were tucked underneath her and a pair of sandals sat on the floor in front of her chair. Her long brown hair was pulled forward over her shoulder, and it looked as though she'd been twisting it together. She glanced at Austin only briefly before her eyes found her shoes.

This was a terrible idea, but Austin opened his mouth anyway. "Do you two want to do something with us this afternoon?"

"Really?" Amber looked at him suspiciously then smiled at Sofie. She knew Austin would not have made that offer without prodding from Dillon, and it appeared she knew why there was prodding from Dillon. "What do you guys have in mind?" she asked.

Austin turned to the guy he'd thought intended to play basketball. "What do *you* have in mind?"

Dillon cast his eyes upward and took a deep breath. "Bowling?" he said, sounding as though he wasn't sold on the suggestion himself.

Both the girls shook their heads.

"How about a movie?" There was more hope behind his words.

Sofie shook her head with some reluctance at dashing that hope.

Amber said, "We just checked the other day and there was nothing good out."

Dillon sighed to agree with her point. "Basketball?"

Something between a groan and a growl came out of Amber, and it wasn't directed anywhere near the person who had said the name of the sport she hated.

Austin scowled right back at her.

"Okay, bad idea," Dillon said, leaning away from the siblings.

"I can't play in sandals anyway," Sofie said.

"That so?" Dillon glanced at Austin and then back at Sofie. "I remember when Austin could talk you into anything."

"Not *anything*."

Sofie sounded defensive and Austin felt a stab of guilt over all the times he'd used a threat, playful or not, to get his way with her. He hadn't tried in quite some time, not because he'd had fewer chances while away at school, but because manipulating Sofie had lost any appeal.

"Fortunately," Amber said, "Sofie has long outgrown any embarrassment over a silly nickname."

"It was a nickname?" Dillon looked at Austin for confirmation.

Sofie looked at him, too. "You really never told him?"

"Of course not," he said. "If I told people, I couldn't threaten to tell people."

"I assumed you'd at least told Dillon though."

Dillon punched him in the arm at the same time, apparently for not telling him.

"I told you he wouldn't tell anyone," Amber said to Sofie.

Austin laughed. "*You* tried to defend me and you're shocked she didn't believe you?"

"I admit it was a hard sell," Amber said, shrugging as though she could hardly believe she'd defended him herself.

"So what was this nickname?" Dillon aimed his question at the group, moving his eyes between them to see who would answer.

Austin's silence had never really been about keeping his power. It had been about keeping a secret with Sofie. Even now, ridiculous as it was, he didn't want to tell Dillon.

Sofie blew out a hard breath, possibly with the last of her embarrassment. "Eenie-meenie-miney-moser," she said.

"Eennie-meenie…" Dillon sort of grunted. "Who came up with that?"

"I don't even remember," Sofie said. "Someone at my elementary school thought it was funny and soon kids were chanting it at recess. They laughed when I got upset. When a teacher told them to stop, they whispered it to me in the classroom." The name seemed a little less ridiculous as a trace of the remembered pain crossed her face.

"Are we going to do something this afternoon or not?" Austin looked at Dillon. Maybe he'd give up and go back to their original plan of one-on-one.

"Well, if you girls could talk *me* into anything…" Dillon lifted his faint red eyebrows at them suggestively.

Sofie returned the look with a smile and a flirtatious wiggle of her own eyebrows, which caused Austin to exercise some significant restraint. He did *not* push his friend over the porch railing into the flower bed below. He wasn't entirely sure why he didn't push him. It sure seemed like a good idea.

Sofie used her finger to motion Amber closer, and the two girls had a whispered conversation. Dillon grinned eagerly. Austin decided that pushing him over the railing wasn't completely out of the question. He pretended to be distracted by the sound of Amber giggling about something as she sat back in her chair.

The blue of Sofie's eyes found Austin for the briefest moment before they focused on Dillon. "How do you feel about treating us to some ice cream?" she said.

"Awesome idea," Dillon responded.

Amber grinned and stood up while Sofie slipped her feet back into her sandals. As the four of them walked off the porch, Austin volunteered to drive. If he was stuck hanging out with his sister, he was at least going to avoid being in a car with her behind the wheel. He'd had that experience a few times, and that was enough.

Dillon offered to pay for all the ice cream since Austin was paying for gas. The ice cream shop was less than half a mile away so that would be an uneven split. Austin accepted anyway because he'd rather be playing basketball and he figured Dillon made the offer because he knew Austin would rather be playing basketball.

A nutty caramel sundae had Dillon's name on it. At least that's what he said before he ordered it. Austin got a scoop of mint chocolate chip and Sofie settled on strawberry while Amber continued to study the choices. She ignored Austin's comments about not taking all day. But when another customer got in line, she quickly asked for the same as Sofie.

They took the treats to a small outdoor table with four attached chairs. Sofie sat in the only place not covered by the black and white striped umbrella. Austin tried to give up his shady spot, but Amber made a fuss about trading her seat instead. This was probably to keep Sofie next to Dillon. Austin walled off that thought with other things he didn't want to think about while he dug a plastic spoon into his ice cream.

"Only two weeks until I head back to school," Dillon said. "What day do classes start for you?"

"The 19th," Sofie said.

Amber nodded.

"You're going to the same school then?" he asked.

Sofie grinned at Amber. "We're going to be roommates."

"Cool." Dillon licked some caramel off the back of his spoon. "I had three roommates my first year. It was brutal. But last year was better."

"And you're still planning to be a doctor?" Sofie asked.

Dillon seemed pleased that she knew that, or that she remembered it, but he sighed as he said, "I think so. I mean, I want to… but I'm looking at all the debt and the years of school and… I guess I'm trying not to talk myself out of it."

"I don't know what I'm going to study," Amber said.

"That's okay." Sofie smiled at her friend. "You're just going to keep me company anyway."

"But if you're only going to keep me company…" Amber gave Sofie a playful look and they both laughed.

"So, um…" Dillon took a bite and paused for longer than it should have taken him to swallow. "Is anyone else going to be keeping you company? Like a boyfriend?"

Real subtle, Austin thought.

Sofie didn't seem to mind. She pressed her lips against a smile and pretended to be unsure of an answer. "I don't think I've packed one of those."

"But you haven't finished packing, have you?" Dillon looked a little too pleased with his own cleverness.

Sofie said something to continue the banter. Austin didn't even hear what it was, but he still wanted to kick Amber for laughing at it. Or maybe Dillon. It seemed that Dillon could really use a hearty kick somewhere. He was eating up Sofie's attention more hungrily than his ice cream.

He asked her about working at her parents' bakery and then talked a lot about himself. It was stuff Austin already knew so he half-listened while eating and had finished his ice cream while Dillon had barely made a dent in his.

There were tiny white flowers on Sofie's fingernails and a purple bracelet on her wrist. Austin thought both looked nice, though it was the bracelet that caught his attention. Dillon asked to see the flowers. He asked as though he couldn't see them just fine from where he was. There was no need for Dillon to grab her hand for a better look. And definitely no need for Dillon to run his thumb across each of Sofie's fingers. Austin left the table to take his cup and spoon to the trash.

When he turned around again, Amber had her trash in one hand and a take-home menu in the other. She tried to push the latter into Austin's hand and said, "What would have been your second choice?"

"My what?"

She quickly tossed her trash and unfolded the menu. "All these good flavors and, um,... well, if they didn't have mint chocolate chip, what would you have picked?"

"What are you doing?" He didn't know what his sister was trying to accomplish, but he was pretty sure it didn't have anything to do with his ice cream preferences.

"I'm just... um... having a conversation." She gave an unnaturally perky smile.

"Really?"

"Really." She tried to brush past his skeptical tone. "Strawberry was good."

"Okay." Austin took a step towards their table.

Amber jumped into his path. "But, um..." she practically put the menu in his face, "the sundaes look good, right?"

Austin took the menu and folded it up. "I don't want to play whatever you're trying to play."

"Boy, you're in a sour mood," she observed.

"I think I'm allowed to be in a sour mood," he said. "I'm on a date with my sister."

Amber cackled and shoved him with both hands. "You are not. We're just... facilitating a date."

"Is that what this conversation," his inflection put the word in quotes, "is about? You're trying to give those two time alone." He looked up as he spoke and saw Sofie smiling at something Dillon was saying. They were fairly close, but the music made them out of earshot.

"Yes." Amber nodded seriously. "Sofie is so nice and so pretty. She should be dating *someone*."

"Really?" He caught the disapproval too late. This was one time he knew he shouldn't be argumentative with Amber. Fortunately, she thought he was disputing the first thing she said and not the second.

"I cannot even begin to express how grateful I am that *you* haven't noticed. But other guys notice Sofie, and I want her to find someone she likes."

As long as the someone is not my brother. That's what Amber was saying. And it's what she'd said many times over the last few years. Of course Austin didn't give a flaming rutabaga what his sister thought of him dating Sofie. But he knew Sofie cared. He knew she'd never even entertain the idea and he assumed that was why this summer had gone so much like the previous one.

He'd come home from school both years to find that Sofie was a solid fixture at his parents' house. But as soon as he'd spent a week or two appreciating that fact and getting plenty of ideas of his own, Sofie began pulling Amber away from the house instead. If he wasn't imagining those sparks to begin with, she was doing her best to douse them. She sent Austin a clear message that she was not interested in causing trouble.

Amber, on the other hand, seemed to be looking for trouble. She stood in front of Austin with no clue that Dillon was the only one who might be grateful for her match-making effort. He had to be the only one. Nevertheless, Austin let her pretend to talk to him for one more minute before he walked around her to return to the table.

Sofie was entertaining Dillon with the story of a sewing project Amber had attempted earlier in the summer. She'd accidentally sewn the sleeve to the skirt and bunched the hem, among other disasters. Amber sort of pouted and sort of laughed at herself as the details came out. It made Austin forget to be in a sour mood for a short time. The four of them enjoyed a little conversation even after the ice cream was finished.

At Dillon's request, he was dropped off on the way back to Austin's house. Sofie had her car there, but she stayed chatting with Amber only a few minutes before she left. Then Austin tried to figure out what to do with himself and ended up wandering through the kitchen while his mom was making dinner.

"Austin, honey," she thrust a wooden spoon at him, "stir this for me while I add the eggs."

He took the spoon and did as he was told. "What are we making?"

"Cream puffs."

"Sounds good." His stomach perked up despite his afternoon treat. "What kind of pudding?"

"Chocolate," she said.

"Not going to complain about that."

She nodded and appeared flattered.

Amber appeared on the other side of their mom as the last egg went into the pan.

"Keep stirring," Charlene Waits said to her son. Then she looked over at Amber. "Will Sofie be back for dinner?"

"No. She's going out with Dillon."

Austin said nothing as his mom widened her eyes at the news and turned them too intently on him. Why would she think he had anything to say? It was none of his business.

Amber sighed and slumped over the counter. "I'm so jealous it's not funny."

Where did that come from? Why was Amber trying to get Sofie and Dillon together if it only made her jealous? Austin still said nothing and tried to keep his own eyes from revealing his surprise or confusion or otherwise participating in the increasingly uncomfortable conversation.

"I didn't know you liked Dillon," their mom observed tentatively.

"Oh, I don't." Amber straightened. "I mean, Dillon's fine. I'm just not *interested* in him. I meant it's hard not to be jealous when Sofie gets more attention in general. She knows how to flirt and stuff and I just stare at a guy like I've forgotten how to talk."

"Honey," Charlene patted her daughter's shoulder, "when you meet the right guy, you won't have to do anything special to get his attention."

Amber snorted. "That is such a mom thing to say. By the way, why are you letting Austin cook?"

It was Austin's turn to snort. "No one is letting me cook. I was drafted."

"Try not to screw it up," Amber said. "I like my dinner edible."

"I like my dinner in a different room than yours."

Their mom sighed loudly enough to end the bickering and continued giving Austin cooking instructions. He did actually eat in the same room as his sister and was drafted again afterwards, this time for croquet. He lost several games due to a lack of concentration and when he returned to the house, music was blaring from Amber's room. He didn't see her again before he went to bed.

He couldn't sleep. He couldn't remove from his mind that picture of Dillon holding Sofie's hand. He couldn't stop hearing her laugh at something he'd said. The clock switched to 1 AM and Austin stopped watching it and threw off his covers. He stepped quietly down the stairs and made his way to the kitchen.

He poured a glass of water and sat on the counter. It was the same spot Dillon had sat a few hours ago while he convinced Austin to skip the basketball. Was he ever an idiot for being talked into that.

The numbers on the microwave kept changing while Austin held his glass and didn't drink much. Watching this clock wasn't any more fun than watching the one by his bed, and he was even less likely to fall asleep sitting up. Yet he did not go back upstairs.

Something other than a noise invaded the stillness and told him that another person was about to enter the room. A familiar purple nightshirt with a kitten on the front appeared in the doorway. Though the person wearing it was familiar, it was not the person who owned it. It was not Amber.

For a moment, it was almost as though his thoughts had conjured an illusion, but her startled expression was real.

"Sofie." He only whispered her name while her hands came up to smooth her rumpled hair. She was taller than Amber and more of her legs were exposed beneath the purple cloth. His eyes traveled down to her bare feet, one of which moved behind the other as though she intended to back out of the kitchen and pretend she was a product of his imagination after all. "I... I didn't know you were here." It wasn't a dazzling remark or even a question, but he needed to say something to get her to stay.

"Yeah, I... uh... Amber wanted me to... to stay over."

"Are you looking for a drink?" Austin opened the cupboard behind him and took out a glass to hand to her.

She came forward and grasped it between both hands, catching his fingers and his breath. She stared at the glass they both held while he told himself to pull his hand out. She had the glass now and he needed to let go even though her hand was on top of his. How did something so soft and gentle have the power to hold his hand so firmly in place?

Sofie smiled suddenly and seemed to shake off a dream as she calmly moved away and took the glass to the refrigerator. She poured some water with her back to him then turned around, still smiling casually. "So were you having trouble sleeping?" she asked.

"I guess."

Sofie put the glass to her lips as she leaned against the opposite counter. "Too much sugar? I heard you had more dessert here after the ice cream."

"I don't think so." He took a sip from his own glass while he told himself not to ask about her date. It was none of his business if she had a good time with Dillon. It was none of his business if she had a lousy time with him. But especially if it was good. He had no place asking about it and no place hearing about it and he didn't want to know anyway. "So, uh... how did it go with Dillon?"

"Oh, I... I had fun, but... uh..." She winced apologetically, apparently about not being excited about the date. Or perhaps about not wanting to see Dillon ever, ever again.

Austin felt a need to relieve her of her guilt and a general lightening of his mood as well. "Don't worry," he said. "We're not that close anymore. You can tell me all the things he did wrong."

Sofie's smile said she picked up on his teasing tone. "In that case," she said, "it was pretty bad. He insisted on paying even though he already bought me ice cream and only told like… three funny stories about you."

"I suppose that whole wanting to help sick kids thing didn't help either."

"Oh, no." She shook her head with mock sincerity. "That's totally unappealing."

"You're just not interested then?"

Sofie lifted her shoulders in a shrug, losing some of her playfulness. "We're going to different schools and all."

That was not the same as being uninterested. Austin wasn't about to press his luck by pointing that out. "Speaking of school," he said, "are you sure you've thought through your plan to live with Amber? That doesn't sound like something a normal person would choose."

"Maybe I'm not normal."

"Maybe."

"And maybe I think we'll get along okay because I don't go out of my way to annoy her like some people." She nodded in his direction.

Austin laughed. "You think I annoy her on purpose?"

"Don't pretend I haven't seen it myself."

"Then don't pretend you haven't seen her drive me to it as well."

Sofie covered her mouth with her hand. Her very amused eyes darted around the corner because she was worried about being loud in the middle of the night and not because she was trying to hide her laugh. In fact, when she moved her hand, she was showing him a wide, beautiful grin. "Know what else I saw?" she asked.

"What?"

"I saw into the backyard from Amber's window this evening."

"And?"

"And I saw you kicking the roots in the badlands. Were they perhaps trying to annoy you on purpose?"

He set his glass on the counter and ran his hand through his hair. It was embarrassing to find out she'd witnessed his rather juvenile reaction to a bad shot. It'd been a rough day, but that was a pitiful excuse. Particularly since she would not let him explain why it was rough. That could only lead to trouble with Amber. Instead of defending himself, he tried to play it off as a joke. "That root has had it coming for years."

She laughed and nodded in agreement. "You may be right about that." Sofie took another sip then yawned as she put her glass in the sink behind her. "I guess we should get some sleep."

Austin reluctantly agreed. He was more awake now than when he first came down. He pushed himself off the counter at the same time Sofie took a step away from the sink. They nearly collided and he put his arm around her waist because he was afraid he was going to knock her down.

It looked as though she was about to laugh at the misstep, but the merriment froze on her face. The flowery scent of her hair filled the small space between them and Austin remembered the feel of her lips from two years ago. It was only the memory of her fleeing the scene that stopped him from trying to make a much longer memory.

But then, she wasn't running away now. She simply stood there, her hand still on his chest where it had landed, searing heat through his T-shirt. The moment stretched and crackled with a hint of longing he couldn't be sure came only from himself. He felt pressure as she used the hand on his chest to push herself away. "Sorry," she mumbled. "That was my fault."

She untangled herself in a hurry and left the room. The words, "'Night, Austin," came over her shoulder with a forced nonchalance.

Right. Like there was any chance he was going to sleep now.

15 PRESENT

S ofie looked at the time, then at Amber twirling around in a dress so fluffy she resembled a sheep. "Eventually," she said, "you're going to have to try on a dress you might actually want to wear."

"You're right." Amber smoothed the ruffles on her shoulder like she was petting herself. "I need to get serious. You pick out a good dress while I take this off."

"Me?"

"Yeah." Amber grinned. "Prove you've been paying attention to what I want."

"I'll try." Sofie walked over to face a wall of white. They all kind of looked the same mashed together.

Amber had said something similar when they first arrived. Then she pulled one out for a better look and said, "Except for this one. It's hideous." She ended up trying that one on to see if it was just bad on the hanger and had tried to hunt for increasingly ugly dresses since. She kept waving off the attendant who was supposed to be helping them by saying, "Not yet."

Sofie thought the woman might be beginning to suspect there was no wedding. She caught the eye of the attendant, who immediately rushed over.

"Can I help you find something now?" she asked. The woman didn't fully cover her relief that they appeared to be looking for a real possibility.

Sofie tried to offer an apology in a smile. "Do you have something only slightly off the shoulder with lots of lace, no beads, and a chapel length train?"

The woman motioned Sofie along the line of dresses, digging her hands and eyes through the fabric and plastic. She pulled one out and draped it over Sofie's arms, then found another that was ivory.

"White," Sofie clarified.

The woman nodded, put the dress back and grabbed another one.

"Thanks," Sofie said. "Let's just start with two."

"I'll be over there when you need me."

Sofie thanked her again and took the dresses to the changing room where Amber was waiting. Amber opened the door to take the dresses and some excited squeaking noises told Sofie her picks weren't too far off the mark. She waited to help Amber zip up the first dress and arrange the train in front of the large mirror.

Amber couldn't hide her excitement as she looked over the dress. "I'm glad my mom decided not to get off work to come with us," she said. "I convinced her we wouldn't pick one without her."

"Really? We're *not* trying to pick a dress?"

Amber cocked her head at Sofie's disbelieving tone. "Well, if we happen across the perfect dress then it'll be the one. But I assumed we would just be narrowing the choices today. I'd rather Mom not get all weepy over a dress that'll stay in the store."

"You say *we* but you're doing all the decision-making. I'm just practicing my patience on you."

"I am not as bad as any of those customers you complain about." Amber almost looked offended, but her eyes crinkled with the smile she was keeping inside.

Sofie appeased her anyway. "No, you're not. And most of the customers are wonderful people, too. But this woman came in yesterday and... well, she came to pick up a cake and complained that it was nothing like she wanted. My mom pulled a fresh cake from the cooler and decorated it on the spot with the woman looking over her shoulder the whole time and acted like she didn't mind at all. Then the woman got all thankful and praised the new cake – which by the way was strikingly similar to the first one – and she offered to take the 'defective' cake off our hands since we probably couldn't sell it with someone else's name on it. Mom told her she could re-frost that part and how we donate any cakes that don't sell so none go to waste. The woman got weirdly huffy about that. Mom told me after she left that she was likely trying to get two cakes for the price of one and that people have done that before."

"I see why you need to stock up on patience."

"Okay, so don't waste it." Sofie waved at the dress Amber was wearing. "What do *we* think of this dress?"

Amber smiled into the mirror. "It's pretty. But I don't think I like the way the sleeves hang down here." She fingered some fabric by her shoulders.

"Take it off then," Sofie said. "Let's try the next one."

"Aye, aye, Cap'n." Amber saluted and returned to her dressing room. Then she popped out a few seconds later for help with her zipper. The next dress had a lower back with a zipper Amber could finish by herself. She came out fully dressed and did a quick twirl before she said, "This one's just not... I don't know. Get a couple more but try to find something where the lace is more drapey."

Sofie took her assignment to the woman waiting to be of assistance. She evidently knew better than Sofie what 'more drapey' meant because she moved along a row of dresses and picked out three more like she already knew where they were hiding.

Amber held up the skirt of the next dress as she pranced to the mirror. "The little girl inside me is screaming at me to admit this is fun. Tell me it's fun for you, too."

"It is," Sofie said. "It really is. Just remember that if I ever get a turn, you have to watch me try on just as many dresses."

Amber grinned and said, "It's a deal." She examined her reflection while she appeared to consider the dress. "Austin came over for dinner again last night. I keep telling him that now that he's a grownup, he shouldn't need his mommy to feed him."

"I could point out that she's cooking for you *every* night."

Amber turned away from the mirror and put one hand on her hip. "Austin said the same thing and I'll tell you what I told him. It's okay for me because it's temporary. Soon I'll be responsible for my own meals and for my husband's." She brought her hands together and smiled. "Although Joe can cook some so I'm lucky there."

Her affection for Joe was clear in her dreamy expression. She snapped herself out of it and faced the mirror again. She swished the bottom of the dress back and forth and frowned as though she couldn't make up her mind about something.

"Anyway," she said to Sofie's reflection, "Austin was all worked up because apparently Monsignor Loy said something to him about me talking about him and he wanted to know what I said. Or what I've been saying." She put her hands out in a show of innocence. "I tried to play coy with Austin, but I really have no idea what the priest was talking about. I'm sure I haven't mentioned Austin any more than offhand comments about me having a brother. I think the Monsignor was just messing with him."

Sofie watched her eyebrows go up as she voiced her doubt. "Are priests allowed to mess with people?"

Amber shrugged. "I don't think there's a vow against having some harmless fun. But I wouldn't be surprised if he had some deep, spiritual purpose."

"A spiritual purpose for messing with someone?" Sofie was beginning to feel weird about talking to Amber while being able to see herself just as well.

"Sure," Amber said. "Like maybe if you tell someone that someone else was talking about him then... then that person might do some soul-searching about traits he doesn't want people to talk about."

Sofie just shook her head at what she believed even Amber thought was nonsense. Then she began to examine the back of Amber's dress to avoid her reflection. It was probably because she was wearing shorts next to a beautiful gown that she was uncomfortable and not the fact that she was thinking Austin didn't have any traits that needed soul-searching. She was about to ask if they could move on to the next dress when Amber softly said, "Sofie?"

Sofie met Amber's eyes in the mirror again and they'd gone serious. "You know I wouldn't care, right?"

"Care about what?" Sofie asked.

Amber turned to face her. "I wouldn't care if you and Austin started dating. I know I've said some things in the past... I mean, I know I would have been just awful about it when we were younger, but I really wouldn't care now."

"Uh... okay." Sofie didn't look up from the lace on the dress. "I don't think I'll be needing that approval but thanks anyway."

Amber's face fell. "I guess you should tell Austin that."

"Wait." Sofie stopped fiddling with the frilly trim and eyed her friend carefully. "Why do you think I need to tell him something?" She tried not to look at herself over Amber's shoulder because she knew she'd see some pink creeping onto her face.

"Well, because... because I think that he thinks that you think that I'd be weird about it."

"I'm not sure I followed that."

Amber appeared to be double checking her own logic. Then she nodded and said, "Yes, you did."

"Let's say I did." Sofie pointed to herself. "I think that you only think he thinks what he thinks because you don't know that he knows that I said what I should not have said."

Amber looked a lot less disappointed and began to smile again. "Now I think that you're just trying to confuse me on purpose so let's go with something easy. If Austin asked you out like... tomorrow... would you say yes?"

It might finally be time to come clean with Amber, but she wasn't asking the right question. Austin wasn't going to ask her out. "I think you're—"

Amber cut her off with a raised hand. "Would you *want* to say yes?"

There it was. That was the question she'd been avoiding for years. Sofie braced herself and admitted, "Yes."

"I knew it." Amber broke into a little dance. When she was finished, she said, "Full disclosure time. How long have you been interested in my brother?"

Sofie sighed. "A while."

"How long is a while?"

"Well, do you remember when I told you that you might think my taste in guys was embarrassing?"

~ 115 ~

"You were talking about Austin?"

Sofie nodded. She felt some relief at this conversation instead of the drama she'd feared.

"So you've liked him for... years?"

Sofie gave a very small nod. She wasn't sure she'd still feel relief if she was forced to admit exactly how long she'd been pining for Austin.

"I can't believe you never told me." Amber's mouth fell open. "Since the prom? Did you start liking him because I made you go to the prom with him? I could give Austin such a hard time if it was my fault. Was it my fault?"

"No."

"Can I tell him it was my fault?"

Sofie had begun to laugh at Amber's enthusiasm, but she stopped short. "No," she said, "you can't tell Austin anything."

"Right. I didn't mean now. But when we're shopping for your wedding dress, I get to take credit for getting you two together."

"I don't... I don't think there's going to be anything to take credit for."

"Come on! You guys were so cute playing croquet the other... Well, you were cute and Austin was just... Anyway..." Amber put her hands on her hips and was momentarily distracted by a loose ribbon. "Talk to Austin," she said. "I know he wants to talk to you and... tomorrow. Come over for dinner tomorrow. Austin will probably show up. No matter what's going on, I don't think it'll make things worse than you avoiding him."

Great. The situation was bad enough and now Amber was involved. Sofie needed everyone to stop acting like something was a big deal. She would talk to Austin, but not for some weighty discussion. She would act naturally and prove to him and to Amber that nothing needed to be fixed. She couldn't fix the way she felt, and she'd accepted that Austin would never feel the same way. No one needed to talk. Everyone else just needed to relax and accept it, too.

"Just talk to him," Amber said. "Tomorrow. We need to concentrate on the dress right now because I think our helper is using up all her patience on us."

Sofie glanced at the woman helping them who was watching but hanging back to stay out of the way. Then she nodded at Amber. "You're right. Let's focus on the dress," she said.

Amber looked down at what she was wearing. "Let's focus on the *next* dress."

16 PAST

C hase suggested a movie. Looking at the options, Sofie agreed. The superhero movie was her first choice, too. That should be a good sign. But Sofie was looking for signs that the date was a good idea and that in itself probably countered any good signs. She wasn't going to think about that. She was going to think about having a nice time with a nice guy. Surely that would amount to something.

When Chase paid for both tickets, that felt like the point of no return even more than when Sofie agreed to a date in the first place. They didn't stop for popcorn or other snacks because dinner was planned for afterwards. He led the way into the theater and up an aisle. Sofie almost walked into him when he stopped abruptly and faced her. "Where do you want to sit?" he asked.

She shrugged. "Anything anywhere near the middle."

He walked up two more rows and put his hand on the end seat. "How about here?"

"That's fine."

Chase nodded and motioned for her to enter the row first. Almost as soon as she was seated, he asked, "Are you sure this'll be comfortable for you? It's not too close?"

Sofie fought the urge to roll her eyes as she assured him, once again, that she was fine. He'd already asked if the air conditioning was too cold in his car, if the seat was tilted too far back, if he should drop her off before he parked, and if the parking space was okay. He was only being nice, but it was starting to make her feel a bit fragile. Or like he thought she'd go Incredible Hulk on him if he made one wrong move.

She began to read the movie facts and trivia displayed on the screen because she was capable of reading and that's all it takes to make giant, flashing words difficult to resist. Guessing on the trivia seemed to help Chase relax. They were chatting comfortably when a wedding scene appeared in front of them and Sofie turned to Chase. "Do you think Joe is going to propose to Amber anytime soon?"

Chase opened his mouth, took a deep breath, and then closed it again while his eyes got shifty.

"I just thought we could speculate," Sofie said excitedly, "but you look like someone with inside information."

He was one of Joe's good friends, and he'd been hanging around with Joe and Amber and Sofie a lot lately. She already knew him fairly well despite this being their first official date. His hair was shaggy and darker blond at the roots, though it didn't look dyed. She thought he was likely one of those people who started with practically white hair as a kid and it grew just one shade darker every year. His eyes were a pale green and gave away his shyness as they were regularly cast down. Right now they were darting among several lower points.

"Come on." Sofie grabbed his arm in both hands and shook it gently. "Tell me what you know."

"I don't..." Chase glanced up and then back down. "Okay. He's been trying to subtly get some info on a ring preference, but he wants to wait until after the summer."

"I wonder why Amber didn't tell me that."

Chase looked confused. "How would Amber know if he didn't ask?"

"I mean about the ring."

"Maybe he was successfully subtle." Chase didn't look as though he believed this any more than Sofie did.

She sort of snorted. "They've been dating more than two years. If he mentioned a ring in any way, shape or form, Amber would notice. And she usually tells me everything."

"Everything?" There was a worried note in his voice before he read a question off the screen to change the subject.

Sofie guessed that he figured Amber had told her that Joe had told Amber that Chase was dying to ask Sofie out a long time before he worked up the courage. She was glad he switched back to movie trivia.

Once the movie began, Sofie felt as though she was sitting in front of Chase rather than next to him. She could tell that he was watching her as much as he was watching the screen. She didn't know if he was checking to see if she was enjoying herself or if he simply liked to look at her. Either option made her uneasy because she wasn't feeling what she was supposed to be feeling by now.

They went to a familiar burger place after the movie. It was familiar because Joe worked there and they got a discount when they went with him. Chase set the tray on the table between them and said, "Be careful with this ketchup now."

Sofie gave him a playful glare. The last time they'd been there, she'd managed to drop two globs of ketchup on the front of her shirt. The first drop was probably the first time she'd gotten food on her clothes in fifteen years. The second was about three bites after she convinced everyone else she hadn't dropped food on her clothes in fifteen years. Amber had laughed so hard she was probably still laughing. "That's not funny," Sofie said. "I still think it was Amber's fault. She bumped my arm or something."

"Right." Chase gave her a disbelieving nod and took a bite of his burger.

Sofie unwrapped her sandwich. "So," she said, "only two weeks of classes before finals. Are you ready?"

"I think so," Chase said. Sofie knew he was being modest. He was very bright, and school was easy for him. "I do have one more project that needs to be turned in but, uh…" He shook his head with a sigh. "It's a group project."

"I'm so sorry." Sofie smiled but her condolences were sincere. She thought group projects could be fun, but she'd worked with a few people that made them a serious challenge. Chase had mentioned his project as though it fell into the serious challenge category. "Is this the same project you talked about before with the guy who won't leave his room?"

"Yes." He ate a few fries and then continued. "We went ahead and had our first two meetings in his room, but there are five of us in the group and his roommate was there both times – once with his girlfriend – and it was so cramped and oh my goodness the smell… We outvoted him and met somewhere else and he didn't show up. Now two people are trying to insist he do the presentation to make up for it but we have one last meeting tomorrow and I know he won't be there and I don't know how they expect him to do the presentation when he misses half the time we're talking about the research but *I* don't want to do the presentation so I really don't know what's going to happen."

"Feel better?" Sofie asked.

Chase smiled self-consciously. "Thanks for letting me vent."

She looked at her fries. "That only works on Joe."

"I know," he said as his smile relaxed.

When all four of them shared a meal, Chase would find a time to move Joe's food when he wasn't looking. He'd just turn a fry box to face a different direction or pull a drink farther away. Joe would give it a weird look and then keep eating. Sofie and Amber managed not to laugh until several minutes later so he hadn't connected the two occurrences.

"Are you excited to go home for the summer?" Chase looked up after asking what he thought was an innocent question.

But going home made Sofie think of only one thing... Austin. She managed to avoid him on most of her visits to Thompsonville, but he was still Amber's brother. He was always a misremembered work schedule or an Amber isn't ready on time away. For four years he'd come home for Christmas and summers and she managed to see just enough of him to feed her feelings until the next time. Then he graduated and got a job in Thompsonville. He wasn't going to go away. Chase was supposed to give her something else to think about, some*one* else to think about, not remind her how soon she might see Austin. She tore her mind away and directed it to her parents, who were safe to think about.

"I'm excited to be back at the bakery," she said. "I talked to my dad the other day and he was going on and on about this new display cooler they just got." That was a good subject. Sofie needed to think about something cold. "He even referred to the thing as his new baby. More than once."

Chase laughed. "Did he send pictures?"

"I know you're joking, but he did send pictures. Wanna see?" Sofie pulled out her phone and Chase looked amusedly at the first two pictures. Then she flipped to the one where her dad had removed the back panel to display the motor, and he took the phone from her hand to get a better look.

They were done eating soon and got in a few more laughs. Chase lived in a different dorm, but he came in with Sofie to walk her to her room. She began to feel anxious as her feet climbed the stairs. She wanted to tell herself that was a good sign, but she knew it was the wrong kind of anxiety. She slowed her feet when her door was in sight.

"Do you think, um...?" Chase rubbed his hands on the sides of his legs. "This was okay, right?"

She nodded and tried to smile. So far it was okay.

"You might be willing to go out again?"

"Maybe... or I mean yeah but..." She needed to clarify that they should only see each other as friends but it was so hard to say words she knew would hurt him. "Sorry," she said. "I'm nervous."

Chase nodded but he misunderstood the source of her nerves. He sort of lunged at her with a kiss. She felt lips and breath and... nothing. There was no emotion even close to what was prompted by the mere thought of Austin. Austin. He was in her head even when another guy was kissing her. That was so horribly wrong. Sofie stepped backwards.

"Goodnight, Sofie," Chase said. He turned quickly to walk away.

Sofie said, "Goodnight," to his back and watched his very light footsteps while her feet nearly sank right into the floor under the weight of this mistake.

He turned back at the corner and waved with an enormous grin before he disappeared. Sofie turned to her door and let her forehead fall against the wood.

It only took a few seconds for Amber to open the door. Her smile faded at the sight of Sofie's expression. "Oh, no," she said. Then she motioned Sofie into the room so she could close the door. "What happened?" she asked. "Was it bad?"

"Not yet." Sofie dropped herself onto her bed and buried her face in her hands. "I couldn't bring myself to tell him it won't work, but I'll need to next time I see him and that is going to be so awful."

"Really?" Amber sounded nearly as let down as Chase would be. "Why won't it work?"

Sofie shrugged. "No spark."

"And you couldn't tell that before…" Amber sat next to her friend on the bed. "I'm not trying to make you feel worse or anything, but you've known him a couple of months and you've known he was interested in you almost as long. You couldn't tell there wasn't a spark before?"

"I thought… or I hoped maybe it was because we hadn't spent any time alone. I mean, he's great. He's nice and he's smart and sometimes he's funny. And yes, I think he's cute, too. There is no reason for me not to like him. I wanted to like him. I tried so hard to like him." Sofie smacked her hand against the pillow.

Amber was quiet a minute, looking away as though it was very important that she pull a wrinkle out of the blanket next to her. She turned back and pointed to Sofie's bracelet. "I still wonder if Austin knew what he was doing when he gave me that."

He'd given the bracelet to Amber for Christmas a few years ago. Amber suspected that he'd picked it out because he'd known she'd feel the need to give it to Sofie to replace a similar one she'd broken, thereby giving her a present without giving her a present. Sofie didn't believe Austin even remembered the first bracelet. The reference now made her laugh, not because Amber was trying to lighten the mood but because she was unintentionally terrible at changing the subject. Thinking about Austin was exactly why she couldn't continue anything with Chase.

Amber exhaled deliberately. "Okay. So every other guy you've been out with, you said there was no spark after only one date. I thought you gave up too easily."

"That's not a secret," Sofie said. Amber continually became a champion for anyone Sofie might date. She didn't hide her displeasure when Sofie said nothing was going to happen.

Amber smiled quickly before her face softened. "I definitely can't give you a hard time about giving up too easily this time and it makes me wonder." Her expression grew somber. "Has there ever been a guy you were excited about, someone maybe you didn't get a chance to date?"

Sofie nodded slowly.

"Why don't you ever tell me about anyone?" Amber sounded more concerned than offended.

"Well..." Sofie searched for honest words that wouldn't betray her secret. "I... I'm afraid you'd find my taste in guys a little embarrassing."

"Don't worry." Amber began to smile again. "You can date a big, fat guy or the nerdiest guy in school, and I won't make fun of you any more than usual."

Sofie tried to laugh. She could not, however, overlook the fact that Amber seemed to think the nerdiest guy in school was a more plausible option than her own brother. Sofie made a decision in that moment though. She was done hiding from Austin. She'd tried for years to make herself forgot him and it didn't work. It was time for a different tactic.

There was a possibility that he'd changed enough that she wasn't in love with him anymore. Maybe she only thought she was and could cure herself with the reality of Austin over the summer. She would let herself like him, let herself be near him. If she didn't find out she was in love with a fantasy, she'd only be in the same boat she was now. It was a leaking, sinking boat, but it would be the same leaking, sinking boat as ever.

17 PRESENT

A ustin began rummaging through his kitchen for a dinner idea as soon as he got home from work. Nothing looked good, and he was sure he was in for another evening of climbing the walls. Everything in his place made him think of Sofie. She'd never even been there. *He* hadn't been there that long. There shouldn't be any memories to trigger thoughts of Sofie, but it seemed his brain was determined to make the most of any tenuous connections.

He'd pick up the remote to watch TV and remember the time Sofie helped Amber wrestle a different one away from him.

He couldn't read a book without hearing Sofie mooing like a cow. It had been a year ago. He was visiting his parents – reading while waiting for dinner to be ready – when Sofie plopped onto the couch next to him and began to moo. Amber had dared her to do it. Because he knew Amber was behind it, Austin had managed to bite back the laugh. He held out until both girls had succumbed to hysterical fits. Sofie had fallen against him, breathless, laughing too hard to sit up.

Even the front door of Austin's apartment – a door for crying out loud – made him think of Sofie. She'd once ambushed him at a door to enlist his help sneaking a birthday present for Amber into the house. It was only something frivolous, but her expression of need was hard to forget. How sweet would it be to come home and find her waiting with some request, something he could do for her?

He wanted to call her right then and insist they have a serious conversation. He couldn't do it. If there was any chance she still cared about him, and wasn't just worried about hurting him, he wanted to see her when she said it. He wanted to be able to pull her into his arms immediately.

Austin couldn't show up uninvited either, as tempting as that might be. He'd love to refuse to leave until she told him where he stood with her. When he thought about it though, he remembered her running away from him at the church and sneaking away from him at his parents' house. He couldn't force her to talk any more than he could prevent her from pretending she wasn't home. Why did she have to keep looking like she wanted him to approach her and refusing to let him? The woman was seven layers of exasperating. He'd have to keep running into her until a good time to get her to talk presented itself.

The worst part was that he knew where she'd be that night. He knew she was having dinner at his parents' house, might be arriving there as he stood staring at cans of soup he didn't feel like eating. The problem was *how* he knew.

Amber had been texting him all day. She'd let him know Sofie was coming over, said she'd try to arrange some time for him to be alone with her, promised that she was a genius at subtle match-making, and threatened to lock them in a closet together if she had to.

God, he thought, *am I desperate enough to accept help with my love life from... my sister?*

The bang echoed around his kitchen when he slammed the cupboard door, punctuating the answer that yes, he was *that* desperate. Just so long as Amber didn't know it. As far as she was concerned, he was only showing up for the food.

He inhaled deeply as he entered his parents' house and went straight to the kitchen as though it didn't matter that he'd just parked behind Sofie's car.

"Hey, Mom," he said. "Smells good in here. What are we having?"

"Austin." His mom looked mildly surprised, but happy about something, as she lifted her eyes from the bread she was slicing. Then a knowing smile slipped onto her face. If she was in cahoots with Amber, he was in more trouble than he thought. Of course, Sofie was in trouble, too. That might be something. "Meatloaf," she said. "I'd have put in the peppers if I knew you were coming."

"It'll still be delicious."

Amber's voice butted in from the next room. "He'll eat anything, Mom. If you want to get rid of him, you have to stop feeding him altogether."

"Who says I want to get rid of my children? We're trying to grow the family."

"Is Joe coming tonight?" Austin asked.

His mom shook her head as Amber's voice entered the room again. "He's working late tonight."

"I was talking to Mom."

"And now you're talking to me," Amber called.

"No, I'm not. I'm—"

Austin's mom stopped him with a raised hand. Then she spoke loudly enough for Amber to hear. "We don't have conversations across the house."

A moment later, Amber appeared in the kitchen. "I don't know why I'm coming in here when I don't have anything else to say to Austin." Her eyes told a different story as they moved in crazy circles, trying to direct his attention to the family room she'd just left. Where Sofie must be. Alone. And it didn't take a genius to figure that out any more than it took one to see that Amber wouldn't know subtle if it jumped up and down in front of her.

None of it mattered because Sofie had followed Amber into the kitchen. "Hi, Austin," she said brightly.

"Hi, Sofie." The whole room changed in a way Austin couldn't describe when Sofie entered. It was simply better. "Are you the reason there are no peppers in the meatloaf?"

"I didn't ask her to leave them out."

"It just seemed best." Charlene Waits smiled kindly at Sofie. "I know you're not a fan and Doug can't eat peppers anymore without getting indigestion anyway."

"Thanks, Mom," Amber said, her face slightly disgusted. "I didn't need to know that."

Charlene shrugged. "You'll be old someday, too."

"Hey! I have an idea." Amber looked at Sofie and then Austin. "Let's play croquet."

Though Amber regularly agreed to play, it was unusual for her to be the one to suggest it. And even if that hadn't been the case, there was something off in her inflection, a forced cheerfulness. Sofie noticed it, too.

She gave Amber a critical look as she said, "Didn't you get enough croquet last weekend?"

"Dad's not even home yet," Austin pointed out.

"I know," Amber said. She turned her head to wink at Austin without Sofie seeing. "Come on, it'll be fun." She grabbed Sofie's arm and began to pull her towards the back door.

Sofie said, "All right," in a confused tone as she let herself be taken outside.

Amber nearly shoved Sofie out the door before she turned back to Austin with an impatient expression. He rolled his eyes and followed them outside. They set up the wickets quickly and fairly close together because there wasn't a lot of time before dinner would be ready.

"Sofie can go first," Amber said.

"Fine with me," Austin agreed.

Sofie nodded and dropped her ball in place. Almost as soon as she tapped it through the wicket, Amber said, "You know what, I changed my mind." She tossed her mallet aside. "You two play while I, uh, help Mom with dinner." She turned quickly towards the house, but not before her devious smile showed itself.

"Amber!" The irritation was plain in Sofie's voice.

Amber flung her hair over her shoulder with the words, "Have fun!" She pulled the sliding door closed as she waved from the other side of it.

While she'd been ridiculously obvious about it, Austin had to appreciate that Amber had done a nice job of backing Sofie into a corner. She'd have to stay outside alone with Austin or be obvious herself about not wanting to be alone with him. Either one would give Austin an opening to ask why.

Sofie gave a nervous laugh and said, "Well, that was interesting. You're up."

She wasn't going to run. At least not yet. Austin took a shot while he considered what to say. The wrong words would have her running for the house or yelling at him again. Her anger last time still made no sense so it might be tricky to avoid. What he wanted to do was pepper her with questions about what the heck was going on in her head. Tension was already radiating from Sofie. An interrogation was unlikely to improve her mood. He needed to begin carefully.

"Don't tell me you just now figured out that Amber is one hair shy of a toupee."

Sofie gave Austin a look that implied he was *several* hairs shy of a toupee. And that was fine with him because she also seemed to relax a bit as she claimed the opportunity to knock his ball off course. Already.

"Man," he said, "you are ruthless at this."

She finally smiled at him. "You know you'd be mad if I wasn't playing to win."

"True." Austin followed his ball to take a turn, wondering if she was also trying to knock *him* farther away.

"Oh, no! You started without me." Austin's dad had exited the house. He was closing the door with one hand and loosening his tie with the other. "Can I at least watch?"

"We just started." Sofie waved him over. "Grab a mallet and take two turns, then you'll be all caught up."

"Yes!" He ran onto the lawn and his mallet had kissed the black ball before he acknowledged Austin. "Hello, son."

"Dad. How was work?"

"Dad! What are you doing?" The second question came from Amber, who had poked her head out the back door.

"I, uh…" Doug Waits looked at Austin, said, "Fine," then called, "What does it look like I'm doing?"

Amber sighed so hard they could see it from several yards away. "They already started, Dad. Why don't you come inside until the next game?"

"They invited me to join."

"Let me guess." Amber stepped outside and put her hands on her hips. "*Sofie* let you play."

Austin watched his dad glance at each of them in turn, apparently waiting for one of them to explain why him playing croquet suddenly seemed unusual to anyone.

"It's fine, Dad," Austin said.

Sofie took her turn to continue the game. "He's playing, Amber."

There was gloating in her voice. She might as well have said, "You lose this round of trapping me with Austin." That should have frustrated him, but he couldn't help thinking it was a little funny. She looked great smiling smugly at Amber.

Amber crossed her arms. "Fine. I might as well watch, too."

She watched Sofie win only about two minutes after the first call to dinner. They got inside before anyone got impatient. After dinner, Amber volunteered to clean up. "Mom, you and Dad go relax and we'll do all the cleaning."

"That's thoughtful of you."

"Call it an early anniversary present," Amber said as she shooed her parents from the room.

Austin pulled out his phone and surreptitiously checked his calendar to see how many days he had left to find an anniversary card.

Sofie and Amber took the dishes from the table and handed them to Austin, who put them into the dishwasher.

"Don't put the pans in," Amber reminded him.

"Right." He took the pan back out. "I forgot Mom doesn't like that. I put the pans in at home."

"Me, too," Sofie said. "Of course, with just me it still takes a few days to fill it up, even with pans."

Austin nodded and ran some water in the pan to wash it in the sink.

"Look at that," Amber said, "he can wash a pan." She was talking to Sofie. "I might have to admit that my brother is not completely useless after all."

"Not completely useless? I'm overwhelmed by your compliment." Austin pulled the wet rag out of the sink and tossed it at Amber's head.

She tried to duck, but it still got her on the shoulder. "Ew," she said as she picked it up, "I take it back."

"I'll take that back." Austin pointed at the rag. Giving away his tool was not the best way to get the pan clean.

"You want it?" Amber grinned as she drew her arm back and prepared to launch it at him. She was only about four feet away. Sofie laughed and her eyes sparkled with amusement.

The rag hit Austin square in the chest with a splat and a spray of water in the face. It left a wet mark on his shirt. He took the dripping thing and held it as though Sofie was next. She thought the whole thing was entirely too funny.

She didn't stop laughing as she held her hands out as a shield.

Amber took her phone from her pocket. Austin was afraid she was about to get a picture, but she just glanced at the screen and said, "Joe's home. I'm going to call him. I'll be back in a minute." She ran from the room.

Austin might have thought he was only lucky except the look Amber shot him at the doorway said she knew she was leaving him alone with Sofie.

"I guess I'll let you off the hook," he said as he lowered the rag and squirted some soap into the pan in the sink.

"Thanks." She leaned against the counter to watch him work, which was surprising. Surely she noticed they were alone. Maybe she thought he wouldn't bring up anything sensitive with his parents in the next room.

He could hear the TV on. They wouldn't overhear. He pulled back a little to see her better since she was facing away from the sink. Her eyes were lowered, watching his hands in the sink. She didn't look up when he stopped working.

"Sofie?"

She swallowed hard. "Relax, Austin. We don't need to talk. You trying to bring it up is the only thing making this awkward."

Awkward was not the word he would have chosen. Confusing? Yes. Frustrating? Definitely. And beautiful. That was the only word left when he looked into her eyes. There was a question there and he didn't know what it was. But no words came to mind when he tried to decide what to say.

Maybe he didn't need to say anything. Maybe a kiss was a better idea. Her lips parted to say something else and he was positive that a kiss was a wonderful idea. If she let him, that would certainly clear up a few things. And if she didn't... well, that would also be clear.

"I almost forgot we had ice cream." His dad's voice entered the room a second before he did. He looked at Austin and Sofie. "Either of you feel like dessert?"

"Not for me," Sofie said. "I may have sampled a few things at work today."

"Maybe," Austin said. "What kind?"

His dad opened the freezer and set a tub on the counter. "Mint chocolate chip," he said as he pulled off the lid.

"Okay. One scoop." Austin returned to scrubbing the pan.

"I think I should actually call it a night." Sofie waved as she said goodnight to Austin and his dad. She thanked his mom for dinner before she saw herself out. Austin was tempted to run after her, even with his hands dripping. But he was stuck on the word awkward.

Awkward was when two people had different feelings. Her blunt statement didn't seem like an attempt to spare his. Did she think *he* didn't care? Was she blind? All the people he *didn't* want to know could see it. And even though Austin was annoyed by all the fuss Amber made about getting Sofie alone with him, he was more annoyed to find he was wishing she'd have taken the time to clue their dad in on the plan.

18 PAST

W hen she put away the mallet, Austin thought she might go inside and leave him alone with Sofie. She was only choosing a different color for the next game.

"I think I'll have better luck with black," Amber said. She pointed the handle at Austin. "Don't even say it!"

He shrugged as though he had not been about to tell her she needed more than luck. Then he glanced at Sofie, who rewarded him with a conspiratorial smile.

Amber was significantly behind after only a few turns. Her ball had been deflected early by a tree root in the badlands, which she had insisted they include in the course. "I am seriously rethinking the placement of these wickets," she said.

Sofie gestured in her direction. "You're the only one who still needs that one," she said. "You can turn it to face you."

"No, you cannot," Austin said. "No moving wickets in the middle of a game, no matter how far behind you are."

Amber frowned at Austin. She pointed at Sofie and then herself as though she was counting. "Looks like you're outvoted." She pulled out one side of the wicket and swiveled it to welcome her black ball.

Austin tried not to let it bother him. Amber wasn't going to catch up anyway. He couldn't quite keep his mouth shut. "Leaving one side in the ground doesn't make it any more legal."

"Not even if she puts it back after her ball goes though?" Sofie was teasing him for being uptight about the rules. They'd had games like this all summer. Amber would get behind, Sofie would encourage her to cheat, then she'd give Austin a hard time for caring.

He might miss Amber a teeny tiny bit when she went back to school, but not enough to let her know. Sofie, on the other hand, was going to leave a big emptiness in her wake. He wanted to talk to her about easing that by staying in touch.

It was difficult to know how she'd feel about long-distance dating when they weren't even dating. Sometimes it felt like they were. She was generous with smiles, and seemed to make excuses to be near him. Surely she noticed him doing the same. But there had been no formal talk, no kiss, nothing that clearly redefined their relationship. They'd been sharing phone calls and texts and she'd definitely crossed over from being just his sister's friend to his friend, too.

He wanted more though and he didn't want to declare that in a text. He had only a few days left to act and that was a calculated move. If Sofie agreed to give him an official status, he'd rather his sister left town before she had a chance to express too many thoughts on the matter.

"You know it all starts with one wicket," Austin said.

"You're winning." Sofie pointed this out as though it was the only thing that should count.

When Austin looked up to respond, the evening sun was catching Sofie at an extremely appealing angle. He forgot what they were talking about.

"Hello!" Amber's voice interrupted the charming vision. "Earth to Austin. It's your turn."

After a few more rounds, it was Amber who didn't seem to know it was her turn. She was studying the positions very carefully for someone with no chance of winning. "Since I have no chance of winning," she said, "I think I need a new strategy. I'm going to join Sofie's team."

"There are no teams in croquet," Austin said. He had a feeling he knew where this strategy was headed.

"If a tree can be on your team, then I can be on Sofie's team."

"What makes you think the tree is on my team?"

"I was actually ahead of you for the first two turns before that big root got in my way." She pointed at the root in question as though it had moved to get in her way.

Austin knew she was being ridiculous on purpose, but he played along. "You were ahead because you went first," he said. "And the tree is not on my team."

Amber ignored him and turned to Sofie. "I think if I abandon this wicket, I might be able to tap Austin's ball and knock him out of the way to clear your path to victory."

Sofie nodded. "Go for it."

Amber tried to line up her shot. She had about four feet to cross and bad aim.

"I don't think you can get me anyway," Austin said.

"You might be right." Amber grinned mischievously and held her mallet out to Sofie. "I'm calling in a pinch hitter."

"What!?" Austin exclaimed.

The two women might have been laughing as much at his reaction as their blatant cheating, and though stating the obvious would only make them laugh harder, he said it anyway. "There are no pinch hitters in croquet."

Sofie made the shot and was about to claim her tainted victory when Austin saw his dad step out the back door. "I can't believe you kids are playing without me again," he said.

Austin shook his head at him. "Trust me, Dad. You did not want any part of this game. It only resembles croquet."

His dad looked longingly at the remaining mallets and balls. It appeared he'd accept even a modified version of his favorite game.

His mom popped onto the deck behind his dad. "Is the game over?" she asked.

"It is now," Sofie said.

"Good timing." Charlene Waits motioned them all towards the house with a sweep of her arm. "Dinner's on."

"What are we having?" Amber asked.

"Is it something that can stay warm for a few minutes?" Austin's dad was still looking at his croquet set.

"Pancakes," his wife said. "And if the kids want to stay, you can leave the game set up for *after* dinner."

Doug Waits looked around the yard hopefully. Sofie was the first to say she'd stick around for a game and Austin agreed.

The kitchen smelled strongly of cinnamon when they entered. Austin saw that his mom had a warm apple topping for the pancakes. The prayer was quick but heartfelt. Everyone was hungry and they ate the pancakes as fast as his mom could dish them up. Soon Sofie offered to man the griddle so she could sit and eat.

"Thank you, Sofie," she said. Charlene moved her plate to the table and looked up before she took a bite. "I suppose it's my fault my own children are not so thoughtful."

"Maybe Sofie's just a show off," Amber said.

"I'll help by supervising." Austin's comment earned him an eye roll from his sister and a laugh from Sofie.

She looked at him skeptically as he approached the counter. "You're going to supervise? Tell me when I should flip these."

Austin had made pancakes a few times, but he wasn't very good at it. "I think it's better if I let you prove yourself. I'll just point out your mistakes."

"That will be so helpful." She picked up the spatula and held it ready to slide under the first pancake. "Is now a mistake?" she asked.

"What do you think?"

Sofie clearly knew that she knew more about pancakes than he did. She slipped the spatula under the first pancake and turned it without answering and without even looking at it. Then she quickly flipped the others and raised her eyebrows at Austin as though waiting for his approval.

"Looks like you might have things under control here," he said.

She kept looking at him, looking as though she was waiting for something, looking as though Amber's disapproval was no longer a concern. If Austin's entire family wasn't sitting a few feet away, he'd have tried to kiss her. Instead, he brought over a plate for the finished pancakes and carried them to the table, claiming the top one for himself.

There was, in fact, a game of croquet after dinner. It was the worst Austin had played in a long time. Even Amber beat him. Without cheating.

"Well, now that Austin is *finally* done," Sofie teased, "I should probably head home."

"If you can stand to wait for me to put this away," he said, holding up a mallet, "I'll walk out with you."

"Sure." She waved at Amber and her dad. "Goodnight, everyone."

Austin's dad and sister gathered the wickets while he opened the gate at the side of the yard. Sofie thanked him and walked through. He called a goodnight over the gate before he turned to walk with Sofie. It was now or never. "Sofie," he said, "only three more days until you go back to school, right?"

She nodded like someone with mixed feelings on that reality. He hoped he had something to do with that. Was she going to miss him?

"I'd like to see you at least one more time before you leave," he said.

She smiled. "You're looking for a rematch, aren't you?"

"No. Or I mean, I wouldn't turn down a chance to redeem myself after that pathetic performance but... I want... Will you let me take you out to dinner?"

Sofie stopped walking and turned to face him. She didn't say anything. She simply looked at him with an expression torn between confusion and surprise.

Austin didn't understand either. He thought he'd asked a pretty clear question and one that should not have come as a shock. "I thought we could get together without Amber," he said.

"Why?"

"We've been getting along so well I hoped... well, I thought we should try an actual date and see how it goes. I want—"

"That is a terrible idea."

He didn't know what he'd been about to say before she cut him off. And he didn't know what to say instead. He'd been prepared for her to raise concerns about Amber's reaction or the fact that she was about to leave town. Neither of those should have made her angry though and she definitely looked angry. She sounded angry, too.

****

Sofie stared at Austin as though he might have lost his mind because it seemed likely that he had indeed lost his mind. One phrase reverberated in her head... see how it goes. He wanted to have dinner and see how it goes. He was asking her out on some whim? Like it had suddenly occurred to him that she was a girl and maybe there could be something between them? If he hadn't found anything after all this time, she knew firsthand how badly it would end for him to go looking for it.

She'd hurt Chase badly, inadvertently led him on while trying to see how it goes. Now Austin wanted to try the same thing with her.

And she wanted to say yes. She knew she'd get hurt, and she still wanted to agree to anything that meant more time with Austin. That part was the most maddening. She was *never* going to get over him. "What are you trying to do to me?" she asked.

"Um..." He looked like he'd been slapped in the face with a cold, wet towel. One that he hadn't seen coming. He clearly believed he'd made a casual suggestion.

"I can't, Austin," she said.

"Is it because of school? We can talk about—"

"I can't have dinner with you. I can't *just* have dinner. I can't just see how it goes. Oh my goodness, Austin! I've been in love with you since I was twelve! I *know* how it goes and I can't possibly do something that will only make it worse."

"Worse?" Austin didn't appear to have recovered from the wet towel effect.

Sofie had a new phrase repeating in her head though... in love with you since I was twelve. She'd actually said that. She'd said it out loud. To Austin. After years of keeping it secret, years of not even telling her best friend, she'd gone and admitted it right to Austin. Actually, she'd kind of screamed it at him. There could not have been a more embarrassing way for it to come out. She needed to hide. Thank God for school. She could not get to school fast enough. She turned to her car without saying anything else. Even goodbye would be awkward.

"Sofie, wait." Austin grabbed her hand.

Somewhere in her head was a voice telling her to stop, that it really couldn't get any worse, but her flight response was already active. Very active. There was no denying it. She jerked her hand free and said, "No. Don't touch me. Don't talk to me. Don't... I really need you to stay away from me. Please stay away."

Her car was still hot even though the sun had nearly set. It was nothing compared to the heat pouring from her face. She didn't look back as she drove away.

19 PRESENT

S ofie sat in her car in the church parking lot. There were
very few cars around her because she was so early.
She'd been up since 3 AM though and couldn't think of a reason
to stay home once she was ready.

A tiny white car pulled into a nearby spot and a familiar
woman climbed slowly from the driver's seat while leaning on a
cane. Sofie exited her car to catch up to Amber's grandmother.
"Good morning," she said.

"Good morning, Sofie. Don't you look lovely today."

"Thank you." Sofie ran a hand over the skirt of her new
pink dress.

Mrs. Waits smiled. "Don't worry," she said. "Austin will
notice."

Sofie snapped her hand away from the dress and tried to
appear less self-conscious and more like someone who didn't
care whether or not Austin noticed anything. "It's a bit cool this
morning," she remarked.

"And yet they'll surely have the air on already." Mrs. Waits
moved the arm not working her cane to indicate the tan sweater
draped over it. "At least I'll be prepared though. Will you sit
with me this morning? That will make it easier for Austin to
find both of us. Unless he's coming later." She cast a shrewd
glance up at Sofie. "I don't suppose you know my grandson's
plan for this Sunday?"

"I believe Amber, Joe and Austin are all coming to the early
mass and staying for coffee." She tried to make this sound like
casual knowledge. Because it was. There had been a blizzard of
texts between her and Amber and her and Austin – and
apparently between Amber and Joe and Amber and Austin – to
arrange a casual Sunday morning. They'd negotiated between

the two mass times with laments about getting up early and jokes about Amber and her precious coffee.

Sofie was proud of how natural and friendly it all happened. She had resolved to quit her childish avoidance of Austin, and it was working. She and Austin were rewinding their relationship to the point before he had a dumb idea and she had a dumber reaction to it. They could be friends.

The large wooden door was heavy as Sofie pulled it open and held it for Austin's grandmother. The building was around twenty years old but it had a classic design and might appear only well-maintained. The pair made their way slowly and solemnly to Mrs. Waits' usual seat near the front.

Mrs. Waits preferred the aisle seat and Austin walked up next to her barely a moment after she was settled. "Morning, Gran," he whispered.

She tipped her head towards Sofie. "Go around and sit with us."

Austin looked at Sofie and smiled as though he was delighted to follow his grandmother's instruction. He walked quickly around the front and claimed the seat next to Sofie. He leaned closer and quietly said, "You look nice today."

Sofie acknowledged his compliment with a small smile and tried to look relaxed. Though all she could think was that she'd have no need of a church sweater with Austin nearby. The three of them sat silently as the church filled with people. Sofie eventually felt a tap on her shoulder and turned to find Amber and Joe sitting behind them. "I like that dress," Amber said.

"Thanks." Sofie turned forward wishing people would stop trying to make her feel as though she'd dressed up more than usual, like she was trying to impress someone.

Sofie felt a little weird about sitting with Amber's family and not next to Amber. She tried to ignore that uneasiness. They were all adults who happened to know each other. It didn't matter how they were connected or who was technically a better friend or that Austin had once kissed her.

Yeah, that last thing shouldn't matter at all. It was six years ago. It was ancient history. It was something she should have completely forgotten, not something she should be letting her memory replay over and over until she could picture him kissing her looking exactly like he did at that moment. She scanned her eyes desperately around the church for other images to put in her head.

Once the mass began, it was easier for Sofie to relax and limit the wanderings of her mind. And she was fairly comfortable as it ended. Mrs. Waits was approached by an old friend as they were leaving and she insisted the others go on without her while she stayed to chat.

Joe led the charge to the parish hall. He stopped a few feet into the large, loud room and turned his head in a full arc of the surroundings. Then he faced Amber and Sofie. "Where do they put the donuts?" he asked.

Sofie stopped herself from pointing as she realized the usual table had only coffee and cups.

Amber said, "I don't see the donuts." She looked a bit confused.

A family with two young kids passed on their way out the door. The dad was carrying a toddler and looking down at a second girl who Sofie guessed at five years old. The walking child asked, "What are we going to have instead?"

He said, "I'm thinking."

"What are we going to have?"

"I don't know." He seemed slightly panicky as she continued to repeat the question.

Sofie made eye contact with the trailing mother. "No donuts?"

The woman shrugged. "It sounds like someone forgot to pick them up but might only be running late." She shrugged again, clearly feeling helpless in the situation.

Sofie also shrugged to her companions. They would need to make do with drinks. The hall emptied somewhat as those who were not making do left the building. Sofie sat with her cup of water and watched the table fill up around her. Amber sat on her left, Austin on her right, then Joe took the chair on Amber's other side and moved it a few inches closer to his future bride. "I can't believe you lured us out of bed early with donuts that aren't here," he said.

"There's still coffee," Amber said. She raised her hand slowly as she inhaled deeply and it looked as though she was pulling the cup to her face with her nose.

"And this *delicious* water." Austin sniffed his cup in an exaggerated impression of Amber. She glared at him while Joe and Sofie laughed.

Then Amber's expression softened while her eyes stayed locked on her brother. "If the water isn't a draw," she said, "we can talk about why you're really here."

Austin smiled back at her challenge. "We went over this last week. It's Sunday. I think you'll find my reason for being here in that list of things called commandments."

"Church is over," Amber said.

Sofie watched the banter between the siblings with less amusement than usual. She knew what Amber was hinting at and was afraid if she kept pushing, she would miss her intended victim and hit Sofie instead. Anything related to wedding planning would work as a diversion. Sofie ducked behind the first topic that came to mind. "We can take the opportunity while we're here to plan decorations for the reception."

"Ooh!" Amber immediately turned away from her brother and cast her eyes around the room. "We're renting white tablecloths," she said. "Don't you think that will absolutely transform these beat-up utilitarian tables?" She tapped at a crack in the side to emphasize what needed to be covered.

"Nice start." Sofie nodded approvingly.

"And I'm thinking the cake goes right there where the donuts *should* be." Joe pointed and then looked at Sofie. "No one will forget the cake, right?"

"We'll have cake and backup cake if need be. Don't worry about a thing, Joe." Sofie smiled at the way his name fell from her mouth. At least she was getting better about one resolution. Now if only she could stop sneaking glances at Austin, who was wearing a blue shirt that exactly matched his eyes, and she'd made a mental note of that at least ten times.

"May I make a suggestion?"

Sofie welcomed the tall man at the side of their table. Austin had caught her looking at him, and Monsignor Loy gave her a perfect excuse to turn away.

Amber also looked up. "Of course," she said.

"I believe the south lawn would be best for croquet."

Amber shook her head at the man with pity on her face. "I am really glad you decided to be a priest and not a comedian," she said.

Monsignor Loy smiled and appeared unconcerned whether the other smiles around the table were a result of his comment or Amber's. "Thank you, my sheep. I believe I made the right decision." He looked at each of them as though checking for problems or needs and must have found none. He began to step away as he said, "You young people enjoy the day."

"I assume you told him about Dad," Austin said to Amber.

She nodded with a slight eye roll and said something Sofie didn't hear. Sofie was too fixated on the priest's parting words. Young people. He'd definitely said young people. But something in his tone or his manner suggested to her that he meant young couples. She felt rather suddenly as though everyone in the room was looking at them and thinking they were two couples.

And they were not. They were two guys and two girls who only equaled one couple. A profound sadness about that fact caught Sofie off guard. She didn't feel like she was going to cry, more like she was going to suffocate. "I gotta go," she said. She waved at the others as she left. It was a brave but futile attempt at deflecting the gracelessness of her departure.

It was late enough in the morning to feel like July, but the fresh air was still a relief even when it was very warm. Sofie walked slowly towards the parking lot.

"Sofie?" Austin's voice called to her.

She wasn't surprised. He was always there. Always. She stopped and waited for him. She was tired of running. It didn't do any good anyway.

"Are you all right?" he asked.

"I think so."

"You *think* so. Do you feel sick?"

Sofie shook her head. "Just… unsettled."

"Sit down and tell me what's unsettling." He motioned to the same bench they'd sat on two weeks earlier.

She wilted onto it more than sat. "I'm just… It feels different being back here but in my own apartment and not thinking about going back to school. And Amber's getting married and Mr. Turner is leaving and I guess sometimes I just don't know what to make of all the changes."

"Too many changes, huh? Is that why you won't let me suggest another one?"

"What do you mean?"

"I mean, is that why you're avoiding me?"

"I'm not—"

He stopped her denial with a highly skeptical look.

Sofie laughed despite her embarrassment. "You *know* why I'm avoiding you."

"No." He shook his head as though she'd asked a very simple yes or no question, and she hadn't asked anything.

"No what?" she said.

"No. I don't have a clue why you're avoiding me."

Sofie returned his skepticism with a look of her own.

"Okay," he said. "I have a few guesses, but I don't know. Is it Amber?"

She'd never seen him so hopeful when mentioning his sister and that was weird. He also seemed genuinely confused by her avoidance and that sent her mind reeling. Had she spent the last year mortified over something he'd forgotten? Or had he not caught her words in the first place? But he had to know. He'd called to make things less uncomfortable. Because he knew she should feel uncomfortable around him. How could he say he didn't know!?

"Tell me it's Amber," he said.

"Why?"

"She's the easiest obstacle because she isn't an obstacle. She actually thinks it's hilarious."

Amber had only known for a few days, and she hadn't laughed. The confusion was helping though. It was pushing aside the awkwardness. "What does Amber think is hilarious?"

"The fact that you're driving me nuts."

"I… uh… Why am I driving you nuts?"

"Because you won't talk to me."

He sounded frustrated and Sofie felt it, too. "What is this?" she asked, waving her hand between them. She *was* talking to him. It was turning into an irritating conversation, but they were talking.

Austin caught her hand between both of his and held on. Sofie relished the touch but knew it wasn't intended to be romantic. Instead it felt... restraining. Austin correctly guessed what she was thinking. He tipped his head to their hands. "I'd really like you to *not* run away for just a few minutes."

Sofie wanted to protest his insinuation that she made a habit of running away from him, but her conscience told her there was truth in it. And her heart told her that if she convinced him she wasn't a flight risk, he'd let go of her hand. "Let's get this over with," she said. "I don't see what good will come of us talking about what happened."

"Maybe none," Austin said, "but I need to know. Do you still... have you moved on... from me?"

He was going to come right out and ask? This was Sofie's chance. All she had to do was tell him she no longer had strong feelings for him and future discomfort would be defused. They'd really be friends. But she wasn't sure she could sell it. Her hand had begun to tremble in his grasp. "Why do you want to know?" she asked instead.

"Because..." There was an edge of impatience in his first word. Austin checked himself then spoke more calmly. "Why do you think I want to know?"

She assumed he was eager to avoid tension, that he wanted to know he didn't need to feel weird around her, or maybe even that he didn't want to feel bad for not giving her the return feelings she wanted. But as she sat there and saw him looking nervously at her and felt his fingers gently stroking the back of her hand, an incredible possibility seemed to be dawning.

"Can you, um, can you at least assure me you're not about to start yelling at me?"

A smile broke free before she could stop it. It let Sofie take a breath. "I'm not going to yell at you," she said.

"That's something." He seemed relieved. "Can you explain to me why you got mad before?"

"Um..."

"Look," he said, "I know you didn't really mean what you said before about… that's kinda young for…" He smiled and Sofie was afraid he was about to make fun of her. Then she realized his smile was more helpless than mocking. "But if you meant you were, you know, at least a little interested… I don't know why it made you mad to find out we were on the same page."

"I didn't think we were. The way you said it, I… I thought you wanted to see if there were any sparks and I figured if you didn't know then there weren't any."

"How could I not know? I feel like I've been chasing you forever." He took one hand off hers and slipped the other around so that he was holding it in a romantic way.

Sofie was unable to talk. She'd told herself for so long that nothing would happen between them that trying to escape her feelings for Austin had become habit, almost instinct. But here he was suggesting that he'd actually been running after her. Why hadn't she seen that? Was it really about Amber, or had she simply been too scared to look?

"Sofie… I love you. Since you're finally listening, I'm just going to lay it out there. I don't have anything to lose. I'm going to be in love with you whether you agree to it or not. All you need to do is let me catch you or tell me to stop chasing you. You don't have to say anything today but…" Austin sighed. "I admit I'm getting impatient and I'd like to know you're at least thinking about picking a side. Can you let me know you're thinking about it?"

Sofie managed to get her head to go up and down.

Austin tightened his hold on her hand. "Maybe you could just give me a hint which way you're leaning?" He widened his eyes in hope.

"I've already thought about it," she said. She'd been thinking about it for nearly eleven years.

"And?" Austin urged.

"And… I'm leaning towards telling you… not to stop."

"Sofie!" He took his hand off hers. "The choices were let me catch you or tell me to stop." He pointed to one side and then the other. "You can't start the good choice with words from the bad choice."

She saw his point and she saw how much she'd worried him, unintentionally. "Sorry," she said.

"You can make it up to me." Austin shifted on the bench to face her. He looked at her mouth. She felt like she was talking to the Austin of several years ago, the one who could get her to do anything with the threat of a silly nickname. And it felt like he was daring her to kiss him.

Austin smiled knowingly and said, "I meant you could make it up to me by never, ever, ever letting Amber think she had anything to do with us getting together."

Sofie laughed because she knew he was kidding and because Amber and Joe had come out of the parish hall behind him. Amber was grinning from ear to ear. Sofie nodded in their direction and said, "I think that ship has sailed."

Austin looked where she indicated. Then he said, "Oh, well," and pulled Sofie from the bench. "Let's continue this somewhere more private."

He led her into the parking lot and let go of her hand at her car before he walked around to the passenger side. She looked at him over the top of her car. "You're gonna leave your car here?"

"Yes." He said it as though he was surprised she even asked. "Where are we going?"

"I don't care," he said. "Wherever you want to take me."

There was amazing tension in the car with them. Good tension. Anticipation. Sofie drove to the bakery because it was close and because it was the first place that popped into her head. It was closed on Sunday so it would be private and Sofie had a key.

As she let Austin in, she remembered how Mr. Turner had said the dim lights were intimate. And she remembered Austin saying he loved her. It didn't get much more intimate than that. She walked to the office, where no one could see them through the large front window, then turned to face Austin. He was looking at her expectantly, but he was the one who suggested they go somewhere. She was having too much trouble believing what was happening to figure out what should happen next. "Did you... Was there something else you wanted to talk about?"

Austin shook his head, smiling. "I've been trying to get you to talk to me for something like six weeks and now you think all you need to do is ask?"

"I guess if we're done…" Sofie turned away and pretended there was a chance she'd walk back out the door.

He laughed and moved to block her path. Sofie tried to move faster and ended up with her back against the outer wall of the office and one of Austin's hands against the wall on either side of her. She was caught in a trap, a trap she didn't feel the slightest impulse to escape from.

Austin grew more serious in response to the proximity. "Where do we go from here?"

She lifted one shoulder slightly. The last time she tried to picture what would happen if Austin professed his love for her, she'd been twelve and a wedding seemed the obvious next step. A little maturity resulted in a lot of uncertainty. "I guess we spend some time together and…"

He lifted one eyebrow. "Talk?"

"Yes." The heat in his eyes said he wasn't thinking about talking though. She wasn't either. "Probably lots of talking." Her hands moved on their own, one landing on his shoulder and one at the back of his neck where she could be the one to make his hair stick out. Her own hair was tingling in the electricity of the moment.

Austin came forward and kissed her lips lightly. Then he pushed himself back and said, "And I might be allowed to do that now?"

She tried to say yes, but no sound came out of her mouth. She cleared her throat and tried to smile. "I think that's… okay."

He squinted at her, not believing okay was her first word choice. "Good," he said. "I'm going to kiss you for real in a minute, but I need to know one thing first."

For real? Her heart was quaking like he'd discovered a new fault line and that wasn't a real kiss?

"How long has Amber known?"

"I never told her about that."

"That? You mean how I asked you out and you yelled at me?"

Sofie bit her lip. Suddenly it was okay to joke about it. And it was even funny that she knew he was never going to let her forget it. "She doesn't know about that. I mean, unless *you* told her."

He didn't deny it. He didn't need to. "That's good to know. But I meant how long has Amber known... that you'd be okay with this?" He kissed her again, lingering a few seconds longer as one hand came off the wall and began to trace circles on her arm on the skin below her sleeve.

Sofie closed her eyes and tried to remember he was asking a question. "How long has she known I..." He'd already said it first. "How long has she known I love you?"

He smiled to hear her say it and nodded.

"I didn't use those words exactly, but I admitted it to her on Thursday."

"Thursday?" He looked like someone who had never heard of that day of the week. "You mean she didn't know anything before Thursday? The one three days ago?"

Sofie nodded. "I never told Amber anything where you're concerned. Nothing. Because I knew she'd hate it. But she was getting suspicious this summer and bugging me and it finally came out."

"I'm going to kill her." Austin shook his head in disbelief. "She had me convinced she was playing dumb on purpose to get me to ask about you. And she didn't even *know* anything."

"That doesn't make any sense."

"Of course not. She's always..." Austin narrowed his eyes in sudden confusion. "Why are we talking about Amber anyway? Did you bring her up?"

"No. That was you."

"Are you sure?" He took his other hand off the wall and both his arms came firmly around her waist, pulling her closer.

The memory of the one other time she'd been in Austin's arms came back, and it felt dim by comparison. The only thing she was sure of was that this was better. The joking, the teasing, the things she usually associated with Austin, they all disappeared as he kissed her.

He kissed her fully until she had no breath left. He came up panting and rested his forehead against hers. "So," he said. "Twelve, huh?"

She couldn't refute it. At that moment it felt as though she had been born already in love with Austin. And for the first time, it wasn't something to fight. It was something to fight for.

~~ The End ~~

www.ingramcontent.com/pod-product-compliance
Lightning Source LLC
Chambersburg PA
CBHW050951120626
46552CB00001B/494